Rainbow Beauty

Rainbow Beauty

Blueberry Wishes

Kelly McKain

USBORNE

First published in 2013 by Usborne Publishing Ltd., Usborne House,
83-85 Saffron Hill, London EC1N 8RT, England.
www.usborne.com

Illustrations copyright © Usborne Publishing Ltd., 2013
Illustrations by Antonia Miller.

The name Usborne and the devices are Trade Marks of Usborne Publishing Ltd.

A CIP catalogue record for this book is available from the British Library.

JFMAMJJ SOND/13 02789/1 ISBN 9781409546238
Printed in Reading, Berkshire, UK.

Chapter One

"That looks great, Abbie," said my sister Saff as she hurried past me, clutching several bottles of nail polish.

I smiled. "Thanks."

I'd just redone the display table with spicy, warming things now that it was officially autumn. I love how the air changes and summer suddenly stops, and you start to think about the leaves falling and getting all cosy and snuggly indoors. I wanted to bring some of that into Rainbow Beauty, so I'd put our Spicy Delight Bubble Bath and Warming Cinnamon and Sandalwood Massage Oil on a rich red, gold-embroidered Indian throw borrowed from my friend Summer's house. A pile of bath bombs sat in a bronze bowl, like delicious sweets. Some were rose and geranium with little rose petals in, and some were speckled with tiny lavender flowers. I couldn't help smiling as three women gathered around the table, smelling the products and chatting about them.

It was three o'clock on Saturday afternoon and Rainbow Beauty was buzzing with clients coming and going for their beauty treatments – waiting on the gorgeous purple velvet sofas in the reception area, browsing all the scrummy products on the glass display shelves, or just dropping in for one of our home-made juices or smoothies. I saw two girls from my sister Grace's class chatting to her as they chose from the colourful display of fresh fruit and veg in the chiller counter – yes, veg! We put carrots, beetroot and spinach into some of our juices – totally yummy, honestly!

To me it was pure paradise, standing there amongst the happy, glowing clients – Mrs. Arthur was flicking through a mag, waiting for her massage with Mum, and Kate was showing off her new perfectly polished nails after a manicure with Saff. Saff was getting really good at nail art now, too. She'd done little rainbows on mine and everyone was commenting on them, saying how nice they were.

Rainbows.

We'd named Rainbow Beauty after "Somewhere over the Rainbow", Mum's favourite song. Looking around me, I felt like our dreams really had come true – it was hard to believe we'd built this place from nothing – well, from a wish, an idea, and from selling Mum's engagement ring which, at that point, was the only thing in the world we had worth selling.

Just then, a treatment-room door opened and Trish, one of our regular customers, emerged. "Hello, girls!" she said, beaming. "Oh, I'm walking on air, I am! Your mother's a marvel!"

"Hi, Trish," we all chorused, as Mum appeared behind her.

"Abbie, you always look so happy!" Trish cried. "And so talented, making up all these lovely products. You're beautiful, too!"

By this point I was obviously blushing about a zillion degrees. And that last bit made me splutter. "Oh, I'm not!" I cried. "My skin and hair are so pale that if I don't wear loads of eye make-up—"

"...it looks like I haven't got a head," finished loudmouth Saff, doing an impression of me.

Trish just smiled at that. "Have you got a boyfriend, love?" she asked then, making me splutter even more. "My son—"

"Yes, she has," Saff informed her. She did a little wiggly dance and sang, "His name is *Mar-co*. And she *lurves* him!"

Grace was walking by with a stack of freshly washed towels, and she and Saff looked at each other and burst into giggles. I did the goggly eyes thing at them to try and make them stop, which just made them worse, obviously. So instead I went bright red and wished I could melt into a puddle of embarrassment on the floor. Perhaps then someone could put *me* into a Rainbow Beauty product – Eau de Cringe, or something.

Trish went over to the old-gold-painted reception desk to pay Mum. "Kim, love," she said, "I'm off on a girls' night out tonight. Why don't you come along? Alison and Denise have been in for treatments before so you'll recognize them, and you'd love Lucilla, she's such a laugh!"

Mum looked a bit surprised for a moment, and then she said, "That's really kind, Trish, but I'm just so exhausted. I've been on my feet since seven this morning."

"Oh, go on, Mum," said Saff. "A night out would do you good. You haven't been anywhere since we moved here – well, apart from over the road to the pub with Liam for a glass of wine, which hardly counts as letting your hair down." She turned to Trish. "Liam's our neighbour," she explained. "He and Mum are like BFF now. There's nothing going on between them, though, what with him being gay."

"Saff!" Mum shrieked. "TMI!"

"I didn't know you knew what TMI meant," said Saff, looking impressed.

"Oh, come on, Mum, go out," Grace urged. "Us lot are all out tonight anyway, so you'll be stuck in the flat on your own if you don't," she added.

Saff gave me a cheeky look. "Yeah, Abbie's going out with…" She went into giggling-and-singing mode again. "*Mar-co*. Who she *luuuurves*."

I swatted at her, then asked Grace where she was going.

"Cinema," she said, "with Saff. We would have asked you, but we knew you –" she grinned cheekily – "had a *da-ate*, with your *boy-friend*." Argh, even serious, sensible Grace was joining in the wiggling-and-singing thing now.

I forgot to swat her, though. I was too busy being surprised. It's not easy to get Grace to leave her Maths books behind and actually go anywhere, and I can't remember the last time she and Saff did something together on their own – they're at each other's throats most of the time.

9

Saff sighed loudly and rolled her eyes at Mum. "Mum, do you want to be sad, staying in on your own on a Saturday night?" she asked.

"I'm going to have a nice bath, a glass of wine, and I'm halfway through a good book," said Mum. "So, yes, please. I want to be sad."

"Oh, but you can be sad *tomorrow* night," Trish teased. "Come out, Kim, it'll do you good."

Mum grimaced. "Oh, I was so looking forward to that bath and book..." We all eyeballed her a bit more, and eventually she sighed and said, "Fine, okay, I'll come out. But if I fall asleep in the corner at half eight, don't say I didn't warn you."

When we'd all said our goodbyes and Trish had gone, I gave Grace the swatting she'd missed out on, and she squealed and ran at me while holding a stack of towels, so we kind of bounced off each other. Then just as Mum was about to tell us off for mucking about, a new client walked in the door and she didn't have to say anything because suddenly we were All Professionalism.

As Mum welcomed the new lady and Grace took her coat, Saff swished off and came back with the juice and smoothie menu and offered her a complimentary drink. She was booked in for an aromatherapy massage and facial with one of our

10

All-Natural Fresh Face Masks, so I went to reset the treatment room. As I restarted the CD of relaxing music and topped up the oil burner, which was filling the room with the delicious scents of jasmine and bergamot, I thought about Marco. I didn't know if I *lurved* him, as Saff put it, but I did know that ever since the first moment we met, I'd had a bone-shaking, knee-collapsing crush on him.

And now he was my BOYFRIEND (sorry, I just had to say that in capitals). My BOYFRIEND (sorry, just had to say it again!). Anyway, now he was my BOYFRIEND (right, stop that now!) I was walking round with a smile on my face like a lighthouse beam. His band was playing at a live-lounge thing in a cafe in town that evening, and me and my friends from my new school were going along. I'd only known Summer and Ben for a couple of months, but it felt like far longer than that. And as for Marco...

Well, us two got back together last Saturday. *Why did you split up?* you're thinking. That's a long story involving both of us being really busy and stressed, but the main thing is that we're together now and this time this is IT, with added foreverness.

When my family and I first got here, I used to wake up every day with this cloud of dread hanging over me, after all the awfulness had only just happened. But now I get this happy glow, and for a moment I wonder why I feel so good inside, and then I remember that Rainbow Beauty is real, not just a dream, and that me and Marco are back together. He's been going all out on the boyfriend front, making me a playlist of songs he thought I'd like, and giving me his jacket when it suddenly went all autumnly chilly on Tuesday, even though that left him shivering in just a T-shirt and the black skinny jeans he always wears, even to school. I wonder if you call the guys' ones that, actually? I mean, "skinny" doesn't sound very manly, does it?

"Abbie, why are you still in here?" Mum asked, making me jump. She was standing at the doorway with her client. "Come on, love, less daydreaming, more working!" she said, ushering me out of the treatment room.

I came back to earth again with a bump as I hurried into the reception area. Grace was looking flustered, trying to deal with three customers, and Saff's next client was standing in the doorway, with no one to welcome her. "Abbie, this lady and her friends were asking about the antioxidants in your Blueberry Face Mask," Grace gabbled, "but I'm not sure about—"

"Sure, no problem. How can I help you?" I asked,

beaming at Grace's customers. My sister gave me a grateful smile and hurried over to welcome the person who'd just arrived.

I got a tub of the Blueberry Burst Fresh Face Mask out of the chiller counter (they look fantastic dotted amongst all the fruit and veg) and let the ladies smell it, then put some of the silky-smooth purple mask onto their hands. "The blueberries have anti-inflammatory properties, camomile soothes, calamine cleanses and the almond oil leaves the skin looking really polished," I explained.

"Oh, yes. Lovely," said the blonde one.

Her friend asked me what I'd recommend for dry skin, so I showed her the Oat and Banana Mask, which really calms and moisturizes. "Oh, and you might like our Carrot and Calendula Hand Balm too," I suggested. "I created it for gardeners, so it's perfect for dry and chapped skin." I gave them wipes to remove the face-mask samples, then handed them the balm tester from our glass display shelves. They loved that too, and by the time we'd all finished chatting, they had a little stack of products on the reception desk. Two of them took the Blueberry Burst Fresh Face Mask and some Rose and Geranium Bath Bombs and the other went for the Oat and Banana Fresh Face Mask and the hand balm I'd recommended, as well as a tub of our Sunset Glow Body Butter and some Zesty Zing Shower Gel for her daughter.

Grace's eyes gleamed as she put it all through the till. I wrapped everything up in tissue-paper parcels finished off with ribbons and rosebuds before popping them into our special recycled bags with little rainbow-print stamps on them, which we made ourselves one evening while we were watching TV.

Once the customers had gone, Grace turned to me. "Great upselling, Abs," she said. "*Alan* would be very impressed."

By Alan, Grace meant her ultimate hero Lord Alan Sugar – although they'd never met, she'd decided that they were on first-name terms.

"I don't know about upselling," I said. "I just want everyone to know about Rainbow Beauty and take a little bit of our magic home with them."

"That's great," said Grace. "And if you could get a bit extra-enthusiastic about the Seaweed and Honey Fresh Face Masks next time, that would be even greater – they're nearing their sell-by date and stock wastage is going to mess up my profit projections for the product line."

"Okay, sis. I'll do my best," I promised. Although we all teased Grace about her obsession with the figures, we knew how important it was. We were a new business, and with around 40% of new businesses failing in their first year, we had to do everything we possibly could to make ours one of the success stories.

Our biggest challenge was getting together the next instalment of our rent – Mr. Vulmer the landlord wanted another three months' money in advance for the shop and the flat, which came to very nearly £2000 altogether (GULP!). It wasn't due until the eighth of October, more than a month away, and we'd already managed to put aside £800 from our first few weeks of being open, so we were feeling pretty confident we'd have it in time. We had to keep focused and stay on target though – goodness knows what he'd do if we couldn't make the payment.

Grace and I got on with tidying up, while Mum and Saff finished treating their last clients of the day. Then we closed and Mum made a round of smoothies with some mangoes that didn't look like they'd survive until Monday, while I got all the used towels and robes in to wash. Saff swept through and cleaned the little customer loo and Grace cashed up. A few minutes later, we all flopped out on one of the purple sofas with our drinks.

"It's been another good Saturday," Grace reported. "Especially with Abbie on product sales. Asking clients on the phone if they'd like any extra bits and pieces when they book has really worked, too. All those leg waxes and eyelash tints add up, and four ladies added a facial to their massage package for today, just because we talked it up to them on the phone."

"That's fantastic," said Mum. "Let's make sure we do the same next week."

"And I did rose nail art for two girls today," Saff said proudly. "It's only an extra fiver, but it all helps, and it looked fantastic. Hopefully when their friends see it at school on Monday, they'll all want them."

"Well done, love," said Mum. Grace and I shared a secret smile. Saff hadn't been sure about doing a beauty course at college at first (she'd been set on becoming a famous singer even though, sorry to say this, but she isn't exactly Adele). It was great to see how she was madly into being a beautician now, and she was really brilliant at it, too.

"We've got some rebookings for next Saturday already," said Grace, "and I'm sure we can fill up the other spaces by the end of Friday."

"Oh, it's a bit daunting, though," Mum said then, "thinking of you all going back to school and college, and me running this place on my own…"

"You won't be on your own," Saff assured her. "I don't have college on Tuesdays, so I'll be here to help, and we'll all be back just after four most days."

Mum smiled, stretched out her arms and caught us all into a hug round our waists. "I know. I'm so proud of you girls. You're amazing. This – everything we've done – is amazing. Now we're up and running, we're just going to go from strength to strength."

"Too right!" cried Saff. "Look out, world, here we come! Well, look out, Devon, anyway!"

"Right, I think we're all sorted here. Let's head upstairs," said Mum, linking arms with me. "I need to get ready to go out before I run out of energy and change my mind."

"Oh, Saff, that reminds me, can I borrow your blue top to wear to the gig?" I asked, as we headed for the door. "Pur-lease…" I added, batting my eyelashes at her.

She gave me a checky grin. "Okay, seeing as you're meeting up with your *boy-friend*, who you *lu-rve*." Argh, not again!

We locked up, then all bustled upstairs to the flat. It looked so much better now that we'd had a couple of months to get settled in. Mum's colourful designer scarf covered up most of the revolting brown sofa in the corner of the kitchen (that, and the telly on the end of the peeling worktop, was basically our living room). Saff and Grace had covered their room in posters (completely different ones, obviously – Grace's were all *Twilight* and quotes from Einstein and Saff had romcom ones scrounged from the local cinema). Still, they hid the grubby, eighties' wallpaper – that was the main thing.

I shared a room with Mum (*Yikes!* you're thinking, and yes, at first I'd been horrified, but we'd got used to it). It looked better since I'd hung some of my clothes up on the walls as outfits with accessories to make it look like some kind of fashion mag's store cupboard. And we'd put the lovely big wool picnic blanket on the bed, since that was more cosy and dressed up than just the plain duvet.

And now I had my chill-out room, of course. It had started off as the manky Hoover cupboard but then Mum, Grace and Saff had secretly decorated it for me, in a warm burnt orange, and added big sequinned floor cushions, fairy lights and a CD player. It was my special place to draw, write, daydream, read – and come up with new ideas for our home-made pamper products, of course.

For supper, Mum had made a big dish of cannelloni the night before, so that was all ready to go in the oven.

"Yum!" exclaimed Grace as we tucked into it half an hour later. "Proper food is back on the menu! You're right, Saff. We're definitely on the up!"

We all giggled at that. When we'd first moved down to Totnes, our fave dinner had been reduced to a tin of tomatoes and an economy bag of twisty pasta. But now Mum's signature cannelloni was back to being creamy and delicious, full of spinach and mozzarella and crème fraiche.

After we'd eaten, Saff put some music on and we all took turns in front of the bathroom mirror (well, okay, nudged and jostled and tried to borrow stuff and complained about each other taking all the space).

Eventually Saff got really annoyed and marched us all back into the kitchen, emptied her make-up bag (well, *bags*) onto the rickety Formica-topped table and said, "Look, *I'll* do you lot up, okay? It'll be good practice for when my course starts. Form an orderly queue and behave yourselves."

"Yes, ma'am!" said Mum, saluting. We all giggled at that, even Grace.

Saff did a really classic look on Mum, with blusher and plum lipstick, and when Mum went off to get dressed, Saff then did this amazing transformation on me. She used my usual lashings of black eyeliner and mascara (I'm sure I've mentioned the headless thing) but with loads of grey-black cream eyeshadow too, and paled-out lips, so I looked really rock chick-y. "Oh, Saff, I love it!" I shrieked, when she showed me in the bathroom mirror. "And you know what would really finish the look? Your black skinny jeans…"

I thought I was pushing my luck there, but Saff was so happy playing make-up artist that she said, "Oh, go on then, and you can borrow my slouchy boots, too."

"You're the best sister in the world!" I cried, and Grace said, "Ahem, she might be the best sister *now*, but Monday morning when you need help to do your Maths homework in the loos before school, I think you'll find *I* am…"

I grinned at Grace. "Yes, I've got the best *sisters* in the world, that's what I said," I replied sweetly.

"Abbie, you don't *really* leave your homework until Monday morning in the loos, do you?" asked Mum then, so I gave Grace a look and luckily for me she promised she'd just made that up.

Grace even let Saff put a bit of mascara and lip gloss on her and we managed to talk Mum up to half ten on our curfew. She made my sisters absolutely swear to be back on time so that when Summer's dad dropped me home, I wouldn't be there on my own. "I'm sure I'll be home long before then anyway," she added. "But just in case there's a queue for taxis or something…"

"Mum, go out, have fun, relax!" I cried. "I'm *fourteen* – I could go and babysit for little kids, and you're worried about me spending ten minutes in the flat on my own!"

She blinked at me. "Yes, I suppose you're right," she said. "I can't believe my girls are growing up so fast!"

Just as we were all about to head out, I dug around in my bag for the little vintage compact that held my home-made solid perfume (my signature scent – geranium and rose) and dabbed some on. Then I slicked a bit of shine onto my lips with my Peppermint Kiss Lip Balm. I'd been wearing it when Marco and I had our first kiss, as we danced in the empty beauty parlour to "Somewhere over the Rainbow", and the scent always brought back that memory. For a moment, my fingers lingered on my lips, remembering… I stood, daydreaming, smiling…until Saff stuck her head round the bathroom door and dragged me out to help her choose the right eyeshadow to go with her slinky red vintage dress.

Mum came back into the kitchen then and I noticed her do a double take at me, and then start giving me a "you're not going out like that" kind of look. I thought she was about to grab the wet wipes and un-rock-chick me, so I quickly announced that we really ought to go. I started bustling everyone towards the door, handing them bags and coats on the way.

Halfway down the hall, Mum stopped still and I thought my cool make-up was doomed, but then she said something that surprised us all. "Do I look overdone?" she asked anxiously. "I mean, are you sure about this top of yours, Saff? Does it look too young for me?" She was breathing fast, like she was about to have a panic attack. "I'm not sure what the others will be wearing," she went on. "I don't know Trish's friends apart from having a quick chat with the ones who came in to Rainbow Beauty. Oh, goodness, I hope we'll get on alright. Look, I think I'll just stay here after all. You go on…" And with that, she turned and hurried back to the kitchen, looking very unsteady.

We all rushed after her.

"Mum, calm down!" I cried. I was really shocked to see such big cracks in her confidence – they'd never been there before.

Saff was staring at her, and I knew she was also thinking, *Is this really Mum talking?* "You'll be fine," she said.

"You look great," Grace insisted.

Mum sighed. "Oh, girls. I really don't know if I can do it," she muttered. "I haven't been out, properly *out*, since…since…"

"What, since Dad had an affair, split up with you, moved out and lost his business, and the bailiffs took our house and most of our stuff from right under us, and we ended up in this hellhole flat?" asked Saff breezily.

Grace and I held our breath. The silence seared and burned around us for a moment, and I felt the pain of it all again, as scorching and sharp as when it had just happened. We looked at Mum, worried she was about to burst into tears and collapse in a heap.

But instead she breathed in sharply and said, "Saff, whatever you do, never ever chat to our clients about their problems, will you? They'd run a mile!"

"Sorry…" Saff half-whispered. "It just came out…"

"It's fine, love," Mum insisted, managing a smile. "And you've put things into perspective for me. We've come this far. We can get through anything.

It's only a night out, for goodness' sake. I'm not being asked to perform brain surgery."

"You'll have a great time," I insisted.

"Yeah, go for it," added Saff.

"And if it's awful, you can always make an excuse and come back early," said Grace.

"Oh, my girls, my lovely girls! Come here!" Mum cried, pulling us all into a big hug again. Then she let us go, smoothed down her top and skirt, and patted her hair. She always did that before she went anywhere or opened the door to anyone. And then she said, "Look out, Totnes. Here come the Green girls!"

And with that we bustled down the stairs, chatting and giggling, and stepped out into the blustery September evening.

Chapter Two

We all crossed the bridge beside Vire Island, one of my favourite places to hang out, and then, after more hugs, we headed our separate ways. I walked up Fore Street, stealing little glances at myself in the shop windows to make sure I hadn't suddenly started looking rubbish or anything. When I got to the arch thingy at the top of the hill, Summer was already there, waiting for me. We both spotted each other at the same time and started running, ending up in a big, squealy, girly hug.

"OMG, you look amazing!" Summer cried.

"No, *you* look amazing!" I shrieked.

"Well, you look totes amazeballs!" she gasped, going totally OTT.

"Well, you look totastically amazeballsacious!" I cried. "Ha, beat that!"

And it was true. Summer always looked good, but in one of her signature floor-length tattered Cinderella skirts, a skinny-fit stripy top and loads of jewellery, she looked like she should have been onstage at Glastonbury. We ducked down the little alleyway that led to the cafe, and even though it was only just past seven and the band wasn't on till eight, there were already little groups gathering outside. I felt my stomach flip over with excitement, thinking that everyone was here to see my BOYFRIEND onstage. (Well, and the rest of the band, of course, I suppose, a bit!)

Just as we were about to go in, Summer said, "Hang on a tick," and then took out the little perfume compact I'd made for her, with her own signature scent of bergamot, jasmine and geranium inside. She dabbed it on, slicked on some Rainbow Beauty Scrummy Strawberry Lip Balm and then produced a little hand mirror from her sequinned bag and checked her face and hair in it.

Huh. That was weird.

Summer never bothered looking in mirrors usually – well, only when we were *pretending* to check our hair in the loos while actually having a girly gossip. She wasn't bothered about how she looked, and anyway, she didn't need to be. She had long dark curly hair that fell in just the perfect place for a tousled, hippy look, dark eyelashes that went on for about a mile and peachy perfect skin. So you can see why I had to wear loads of make-up to look even *vaguely* non-hideous next to her.

"You're making an effort," I teased. "For anyone special?"

As soon as I'd said it, I kind of wished I hadn't. I'd promised myself I wouldn't get involved in Summer's love life. Not since the whole awkward, embarrassing, off-the-cringe-scale beach-party situation. (Basically, she'd had a crush on Ben for a while, and, playing matchmaker, I'd gone over at the party to tell him how she felt. But somehow, just as I was about to say she liked him, he'd got the wrong end of the stick and tried to kiss *me* instead. Which, as you can imagine, was basically AWFUL, for all of us. It's sorted now, though – the boys didn't kill each other, Ben wasn't really into me and Summer's not into Ben any more.)

Luckily, she just smiled at me and said, "Why would it be *for* anyone? Girls should enjoy looking good to feel good for themselves, not for boys."

"OMG, you sound like Grace!" I cried.

"Is she coming?" she asked.

"No, she's gone to the cinema with Saff." I smiled to myself, imagining them standing in the foyer right at that moment, bickering about which film to see.

"Oh, that's great," said Summer. "Her getting out more, I mean."

"Yeah, we're all out at once, for the first time in ages, even Mum," I said. "And you're right – it does feel great. Like we're getting back to normal – well, a new kind of normal, anyway."

Summer gave me a big smile and linked arms with me. Then we headed into the cafe, which looked gorgeous, with fairy lights glowing against the bare brick walls, and little tea-light candles in jars everywhere. The tables had been pushed back to the edges of the room and the band's gear was set up in one corner. People were sitting on some of the tables, or standing around chatting. We went up to the counter to get some drinks and Summer talked to the owner, Pete – she seemed to know every single person in Totnes. When we came to pay, I found my mouth loudly announcing to him that I was the GIRLFRIEND of the guitarist. Yikes!

Summer smirked. "You've got it bad, haven't you?"

"It's not me, it's my mouth!" I cried. "I have *no* control over it, like *zero*."

We crossed the room and spotted Ben, who was wearing his Scooby-Doo T-shirt as usual, and chatting to his footie mates.

"Hiya," I said, as we reached him.

"Hey."

We hugged, and I thought he and Summer would hug too, but instead they just did that little "hi" wave thing. Okay, so maybe things were still a *teeny bit* awkward between them after the beach party.

"I thought you weren't getting here till later," I said, "what with Gabe's bedtime."

"Nah, Dad's just back from Germany, so I skipped off early," he told us. Ben helped out with his two-year-old brother a lot. Having a toddler in the family meant things were pretty hectic, especially when his dad, a long-distance lorry driver, was away.

"Cool," I said. "Right, I'm off to say hello to Marco backstage." I swanned off in Saff's slouchy boots, thinking that if things *were* still a bit strained between Summer and Ben, the quicker they spent a bit of time alone together, the quicker it would be sorted.

"Backstage" turned out to be a little stockroom next to the loos where Marco was standing with Tay,

Chaz and Declan, the rest of the band. He was leaning on a cash-and-carry-sized box of biscotti and talking through their set list. Two girls, who I recognized as Shalini and Jas, Declan and Chaz's girlfriends, were chatting by a stack of egg-free mayo jars, while listening to an iPod between them. They smiled at me as I walked in and I did a massive grin back, then toned it down a bit and tried not to look completely uncool.

When I said "hi" to the band guys, they did the traditional boy greetings of grunt, slight hand wave and mumble.

"Hey," said Marco, giving me a smile.

My stomach flipped over and my knees actually buckled a bit under me and I thought I was going to have to hang on to the shelf of organic orange juice cartons to avoid falling in a jelly-legged heap on the floor. However often I saw him, Marco still seemed to have that effect on me. It took me a while to get used to him, so that I wasn't just staring at his dark blue eyes and mop of black curls with my mouth hanging open. He caught me into a hug, and electricity buzzed between us, the same way it had when we'd first met, when he'd pulled me out of a storm into a doorway, and put his blazer round my shoulders. I was swirled up in his cinnamon, musk and cedar wood smell all over again and I had to actually *force* myself to put him down. "How's it going?" I asked.

"Good, yeah. We were just sorting out a few last-minute things. You look really nice, by the way."

"Thanks," I said, and clamped my lips shut before my uncontrollable mouth started going on about me being headless if I don't wear loads of make-up...

"You know Shalini and Jas, don't you?" he asked.

The girls gave me another smile and chorused "Hi".

"Hi," I said.

"I like your top," said Shalini.

And I almost did the mad-person grin again. I stopped myself just in time and managed to do a normal smile instead and say, "Thanks, it's my sister's."

"I'll come out and see Ben," Marco said. "We're pretty much done here, anyway."

The boys did that whole laterz-and-back-slapping thing, even though they were seeing each other in about ten seconds' time, and then Marco followed me back down the little corridor, holding my hand. He only let go because he saw Ben and of course they did the complicated high-five thing that all boys have to do. (They do it instead of the hugging and cheek-kissing and squealing "OMG, you look amazing" to each other that girls do.)

Lots of the people who'd been meeting up outside had come in by then, and I spotted Amany and Iola from Art Club. Some of Tay, Chaz and Declan's mates were there too, and Selima, Alex and Raven (I know – SO Totnes hippy-style to call your kid that!) from Media. There was a buzz of chatter round the room, and loads of the girl-hugging and boy-high-fiving thing was going on as friends found each other.

I recognized a group of girls who we used to call Marco's Year 8 Fan Club (about to be his Year 9 Fan Club). He used to flirt with them when they came over to our table in the canteen at school and stuff, and me and Summer always teased him about it and killed ourselves laughing.

Strangely enough, it didn't seem all that funny now that I was his girlfriend. I started to worry that somehow just seeing them would make him go back to his old flirty ways, but when they came up to us, he hardly spoke to them, apart from to be polite. Actually, they seemed to talk to me more than him, saying they'd heard we were together and asking how it happened, and then going "Aww!" and "Wow!" and "Soooo romantic!" when I told them (while he stood there blushing, then sidled away – hee hee).

As Pete went by, he stopped and said to Summer, "Oh, I meant to ask, are you doing the Autumn Fayre at your place again this year? It was great fun last time."

"Yeah, on the seventeenth," she told him. "As in, not this Saturday but next. Mum's about to ring you."

"Put Sue and me down to volunteer. We'll do a mobile cafe again – it raised quite a bit last time."

Summer grinned at him. "Thanks, Pete, I'll let her know."

"Oh, yeah, the Fayre," I said, remembering that Summer had mentioned it a couple of weeks back. "You still haven't let me know what I can do." They put on a hog roast, raffle and stalls in their garden, all in aid of the local cancer hospice.

"Don't worry, you're on Mum's list of happy helpers," she told me. "And, by the way, I'm impressed," she said, gesturing after the Marco Fan Club, who were heading off to the loos. "You know I've had my doubts about Marco as boyfriend material, but he hardly even noticed them."

I tried hard not to say, *I told you so*. Then, "I told you so," I said, because of my unstoppable mouth.

Ben came up just then. "I was talking to Pete about the Autumn Fayre," he said. "Put me down to help with the hog roast."

"You're on Mum's list as well," Summer told him, smiling. "But I'm not sure if she's given out the jobs yet. I'll ask her. And *you're* down to help out too," she called over to Marco. "Hey, maybe we could sell your autograph for a fiver a time!"

"Make it ten, and you're on!" he called back, and pulled a face at her.

Summer swatted the air, pretending it was his head. Those two had known each other for so long they acted like brother and sister – including arguing and taking the mickey out of each other at all times. Marco gave me a smile, and headed over to the stagey bit where the rest of the band had gathered. Then they began to get sorted out and tune up.

A few minutes later, a hush fell over the crowd as Headrush started to play. I absolutely loved watching Marco onstage – I mean, licence to stare or what?! I loved the concentration on his face, the way he moved to the music, his hair flopping around in time to the beat. I leaned against a table and settled back to enjoy it all. And just when I thought it couldn't get any better, Declan handed the mic to Marco. My BOYFRIEND cleared his throat and gave me a slightly embarrassed smile and said, "I wrote this for you, Abbie."

Well, *everyone* turned to look at me and I was so

shocked that I stood bolt upright and slopped apple juice down myself. Oh, well. I guess I knew that Saff's clothes could only make me *look* cool, not act it.

"Ahem," said Tay, raising his eyebrows at Marco.

"Okay, Tay helped a bit with the lyrics. I'm not going to force you lot to listen to me sing it, but I want Abbie to know it's from me to her."

"Ahhh!" went most of the girls in the room, and I saw Shalini and Jas beaming at me. Ben pretended to be sick, so I slapped him one, and only a couple of Marco's Nearly Year 9 Fan Club looked like they wanted to kill me. Most of them seemed to think it was the most romantic thing they'd ever heard.

So the band played my song, and I'm not going to write the lyrics down here but to give you a rough idea it was going on about "that new girl" and "seeing that girl" and "wanting to get to know that girl" and stuff. Anyway, it was really good, and if I'd heard it on the radio and it hadn't been about me I would still have thought it was really good.

When it had ended and they'd gone on to something rocky, I thought it was safe to move my eyes from the stage and risk looking around (I'd been too embarrassed to do that when the song was playing, in case anyone thought I was being, like, *Oh yes, I am sooooo that girl, check me out!*). All my new friends were there, my gorgeous boyfriend was on the stage and had written a song for me, and my family was safely out having a good time. A ripple of pure happiness ran through me. Amazingly, even after all we'd been through, I really felt that things couldn't get much better.

Chapter Three

On Sunday morning we all woke up late and eventually gathered in Rainbow Beauty for our weekly meeting. Over the holidays we'd been leaving it until Monday, but we couldn't do that any more as Grace and I started back at school the next day. We usually looked at which products we needed to make more of in the coming week, and what had to be ordered in, like leg wax or nail files. We also deep-cleaned the treatment rooms, sorted out the washing and took any fruit and veg that was looking a bit past its best upstairs to make soups and fruit salads.

And this week, we started off talking about our nights out.

"So much for being asleep in the corner at half eight," Saff teased, as Mum walked in. "You didn't get in until nearly midnight!"

"I hope *you* were back on time—" Mum began.

"Summer's dad dropped me home at about twenty past ten, and Saff and Grace were in a few minutes after me, bang on half ten as promised," I reported truthfully.

"So how was it?" Grace asked Mum.

Mum smiled. "I'm really glad I went," she said. "Trish's friends are lovely and we had a real laugh. Did you girls enjoy yourselves?"

Of course, as predicted, Saff and Grace hadn't been able to decide on a film and had tossed a coin for it in the end, before they killed each other. And when I told them all about Marco writing the song for me, Mum and Saff dissolved into girly squeals and even Grace couldn't help smiling, before saying how objectifying of women the whole thing was, of course.

Just then the bell over the door jangled and Liam walked in. He was looking extra muscly and tanned after a summer spent swimming in the sea (and a week clubbing in Ibiza). "Ooooh, Kim, you dirty stop-out!" he cried. "What time did *you* get in last night?!"

Mum grinned at him. "You only *know* I was out because you got in right after me!" she said.

He beamed back. "I've come to look at that leaky pipe," he told her. "I should be able to do something with it – otherwise I'll get my mate Gordon to come and look tomorrow on his way home." Liam was a builder, and had done the shop fit for us for just the cost of the materials. He'd got Gordon to plumb in our washing machine for free too. It was fair to say that, without Liam and his mates in the building trade, Rainbow Beauty would have stayed just a dream.

"Oh, Liam, you're a lifesaver," said Mum. "Let me know when you've got a spare hour and I'll book you in for a massage in return."

Liam smiled. "Now *you're* the lifesaver!" he told her.

Then he stayed to chat for a while. He asked Grace and I how we were feeling about school starting again (answer: me – excited about seeing Marco every day; Grace – excited about Maths Club and the unlimited studying opportunities in general). Then he fixed the pipe, and had just left when the phone rang.

We knew it would be Dad – he'd arranged to call while we were having our meeting so that he could chat to us on the landline.

I raced to be the one to pick up. "Hi, Dad," I cried. "How are you?"

"Good, thanks," he said. "Well, missing you all something rotten, but keeping busy. You?"

"My life is fairly nice, thank you," I announced, ignoring Saff's sniggers. "Apart from missing you, of course."

"Well, good," he said. "I'm just calling with an update on how things are going this end." Dad, Grace and I had been on a crazy, roller-coaster sales drive in Kensington and Chelsea over the summer, showing London boutiques our specially created Beauty and the Beach range. Dad had been in charge of delivering the products they'd ordered too.

"Hold on," I said. "Right, now you're on speakerphone."

"Cool. Hi, girls!" called Dad.

"Hi, Dad," my sisters chorused.

Mum came back in and I was about to mention that she was there too when she put a finger to her lips and cupped her ear, which I took to mean that she just wanted to listen in. I thought that was probably a good idea, considering the way she and Dad always started arguing whenever they tried to talk to each other. Grace had been really upset by them fighting before, when Dad had come down to

40

see us, and Mum probably didn't want to risk it happening again.

"Well, I've got some good news," Dad was saying. "I've been back into the shops we sold to, to get feedback, and their customers *love* the Beauty and the Beach stuff. It won't be long before it's all sold through, and I'd like to go back soon and offer them something else. Of course, they won't want more of the summer-themed products, not with the seasons changing, but perhaps you could come up with something autumnal?"

"We *could*," I began, my mind whirring as I spoke, "but then we'd just have the same issue of having to change the product range with the next season."

"Beauty and the Beach was great!" cried Saff.

"Oh, I know," I said quickly. "And it was the right thing to go in with at first, because a seasonal range was different and irresistible to the shops. But now we've got our foot in the door, I think we should offer them a core Rainbow Beauty range."

"Good idea," said Dad. "That way we can make sure we're in the shops all year round."

"I agree," said Grace. "And we can always introduce themed ranges and one-off special products later."

"We'll have a think about which products to

include and send you some samples to show to the shops. How does that sound?" I asked him.

"Great!" said Dad. "You're doing such an amazing job, girls. I can't tell you how proud I am."

I quickly glanced at Mum and saw that she was smiling a little.

"Grace is going in for Young Apprentice next year," Saff teased.

"She should," said Dad. "She'd win, I bet."

Grace absolutely glowed at that, which was nice, seeing as she wasn't even *speaking* to Dad only a couple of weeks ago (and had said that she never wanted to see him again and didn't care about him). Then they had to talk about the new website they were putting together, and it was lovely to listen to them. The site was to showcase products for the London shop managers, who'd be able to request samples and order online. All that had been made possible because Dad had been loaned a laptop by a charity that helped people get back on their feet. And Liam had given us his old one, as he was upgrading anyway. It was already set up on his broadband, which he said we could use to save money. That was great – as Grace said, it was another £40 a month towards our rent money for the October deadline.

"Yippee! We're going global!" Saff cried, dancing around.

Dad laughed. "Well, I wouldn't go that far, but we could certainly go national!"

I glanced at Mum, thinking she'd have something to say about him using the word "we". She'd made it more than clear to him that Rainbow Beauty was ours – me, her, Grace and Saff's – and that he was just the delivery man. But if she was annoyed, she wasn't giving anything away.

"Great. Let's get the ball rolling then," said Dad. "When you get this core product range together, we could start with that. As soon as it's finalized, I'll get a web page up, and meanwhile I'll find out about the legal wording we need, and what our returns policy should be, and things like that. Oh, and I've been thinking about expanding the London shop sales. I'm looking at other areas with a similar profile to Kensington and Chelsea – Marylebone, for example..."

"Ooooh, bags I come to the pitches with you," said Saff, her eyes lighting up. "I love the little shops on Marylebone High Street."

"Well, I guess if your mum can spare you..." Dad began.

Saff was about to ask her, but Mum waved her hands at her and put her finger to her lips. She obviously still wanted to pretend she wasn't there. "Yes, I'll have to check with her, when she's here, which she isn't," said Saff, more woodenly than an oak tree. She really is the worst actress in the world.

"Okay, well, I was thinking, once the core range goes into the shops here and we've got some good sales figures behind us, and perhaps an endorsement or two, I want to approach some bigger stores," said Dad. "Liberty has a reputation for showcasing small, artisan suppliers, and Selfridges—"

"What? You mean the massive one…on Oxford Street?" I gasped, staring at the phone with my eyes goggling out.

Dad laughed. "Yeah, Abs, I mean the blooming great giant one. Think BIG, girls!"

Us three got really giggly and over the top then, thinking that we could end up with this massively famous beauty brand. And that's when Mum finally spoke. "Well done, Al," she said simply.

"Kim?" stuttered Dad, sounding a bit startled. "I didn't realize you were there. I hope you don't think I'm interfering. All these things are just ideas…" He trailed off, probably waiting for Mum to give him an earful about how it was *our* business and he could keep his lying, cheating hands off it. We were all waiting for it too.

But actually, she just said, "Not at all. You're doing good work." We all stared at her as if she'd been replaced by someone else. Then she pursed her lips and added, "If only you'd been this proactive when your own business was on the ropes, instead of burying your head in the sand and going off with that *bimbo*, perhaps—" There, that was more like it.

I gave her a sharp look and she stopped herself, probably remembering how she'd upset Grace before. She sighed. "Look, Al, just go for it, that's what I'm saying," she finished.

"Right. Thanks. Great. I will, then," said Dad, sounding bewildered, but pleased.

"Dad, I could really do with coming up to see you soon," said Grace. "We need to go over all this web stuff face-to-face."

"And I'd like to go through our new core range with you when we've got it sorted," I added, jumping in. "Make sure you're up to speed for pitches."

"If you two are going to London, I'm coming," Saff told us. "I haven't seen my mates since we moved down here."

"Hang on!" cried Mum. "*No one* is going to London. It'd have to be a weekend because of school and college, and I really need all of you at Rainbow

Beauty on Saturdays, especially you, Saff – you've got clients booked in."

"Oh, come on, Kim, it's one day," Dad grumbled. "I'm desperate to see my girls."

I cringed, waiting for Mum to go mad. But instead she took a deep breath and said, "They'd have to go up on Saturday and come back Sunday, so it'd be a whole weekend, *actually*, Al. And I'll be really rushed off my feet here as it is."

We all gave her pleading, puppy-dog looks.

"Oh, please, Mum," said Saff. "We haven't seen Dad for ages."

Dad, sensibly, was silent.

Mum sighed. "Look, I'm not trying to come between you girls and your dad," she said. "And it's true that you need to sort the online side of things out together, Grace. I suppose you can all go up on the early coach this Saturday. I'll manage – it's only for one day. You'll need to ask Emily to cover for you on the manicure side, Saff. I can't pay her much, though." Saff had met Emily at the college open day and they were about to start the beauty course together.

Saff leaped onto her, squealing, "Thanks, Mum! You're a legend! And Emily won't want any money – she's just desperate for more experience."

Grace looked really pleased too, but I felt torn. I didn't want to leave Mum on her own, but I was desperate to see Dad. I just missed him so much. I always have, ever since he left, even though I was angry with him every single day at first (and I still am a lot of the time). I turned to Mum, about to say that I wouldn't go, but she saw the look on my face and said firmly, "You go, Abbie. I'll be fine."

"Thanks, Kim," said Dad.

Mum didn't say anything back, but she nodded slightly.

After we'd all said goodbye to Dad and hung up, we talked about what to create for the London shops. Saff started talking about a citrus theme, and Grace wondered whether we could showcase different essential oils. I was just staring down at the little rainbows painted onto my nails and listening to them argue about which was better when I realized that we already *had* a signature theme – I mean, we were *called* Rainbow Beauty, after all!

"Rainbows, of course!" I cried. "We can have one product for each colour, and put them in gift kits in rainbow order as well as selling them individually. I'm sure we can find something for each, even if we have to fiddle around with the colourings a bit to get them perfect."

"Fab idea!" said Saff. "Much better than *essential oils*."

"Much better than *citrus*," Grace snapped back.

We all started throwing ideas around while Grace frantically scribbled down notes. In the end, we settled on Spicy Delight Bubble Bath for red. It was already pinkish, but we were planning to experiment with alkanet, a natural colouring, to make it really bright and cheerful.

For orange we went for our Carrot and Calendula Hand Balm, which always flew off the shelves at Rainbow Beauty. "It's for gardeners – is that a bit specific?" Mum asked, with a frown.

"We could change the description and take the gardening bit out and just say it's good for dry, chapped skin," I suggested. "And we'll have to add turmeric and paprika to make it really orange."

"Great," said Grace, scribbling it all down.

"Yellow's easy," said Saff. "Our Zesty Zing Shower Gel." She obviously wasn't going to let go of the citrus theme. But actually I agreed with her. It was one of our most popular products already thanks to its huge burst of lemon, mandarin and grapefruit – perfect for getting even the biggest sleepyhead going in the morning.

For green we settled on the Olive Grain Foot

Scrub, and decided to experiment with blue camomile and turmeric to make it even more vibrant than it already was. And blue camomile would also turn our lovely blue Chest-Clearing Massage Oil Blend (made with eucalyptus, peppermint, lavender, tea tree, rosemary and thyme oils) the perfect colour.

"Right. Indigo next," said Mum.

"What *is* indigo, anyway?" asked Saff, wrinkling up her nose. "I've always wondered that."

As Grace tutted and rolled her eyes, I went over to the chiller counter and came back with a punnet of blueberries. "These, look," I said.

Saff peered at them. "Oh, right. I thought they were just *blue*, you know, being called *blue*berries."

"I guess indigo is a kind of purply-blue," I said.

"We don't have anything that colour," said Mum. "Well, nothing that would work, anyway. We can't sell our Blueberry Burst Fresh Face Mask to the London shops because it needs to be refrigerated."

I frowned. "You're right. Maybe we could make something else up, though. Blueberry oil is great for dry skin, and we haven't got a body butter in the London range at the moment. Obviously we can't transport fresh blueberries, so we'd have to use fragrance oil to get the yummy smell. I'm sure we could experiment with our natural colourings to get a good indigo colour, though."

"That sounds gorgeous," said Saff, "and we can use shea butter to make it really indulgent."

We all agreed on the body butter and then moved on to violet. That was easy – Lavender Bath Bombs with real lavender flowers. They'd always been a good seller for us and the flowers made them look great. And in the end we decided to call each product simply Red, Blue or whichever colour, so that the range had a strong identity and the rainbow theme really stood out. We would put the full product name underneath that, in much smaller writing.

I put the kettle on for coffees then and Mum popped out to get some croissants from the corner shop. I was just walking back through from the kitchenette with the tray of mugs when she came back in. She was looking really shaky and pale, and instead of a bag of croissants she was clutching a leaflet.

"Oh no, didn't they have any left?" Saff said.

"Are you okay?" Grace asked.

Suddenly a really bad feeling came over me, like a darkness swooping down and settling right in the centre of my chest. "Mum?" I croaked. "What is it?"

But she didn't speak. Instead, she lurched over to

the purple velvet sofas and Grace had to sit her down. It looked like she was in shock.

The blackness deepened around me then and I put the tray down before I dropped it. "Mum, what's happened? Has there been an accident?" I gasped.

She came round then. She shook her head slightly and then passed me the leaflet. Her hands were trembling.

I took in what it said (and why Mum was so upset) in one glance. And then I couldn't speak either.

"Oh, for goodness' sake," Grace snapped, snatching the leaflet from me. "What can be so awful that...oh."

"What?" Saff demanded. "Come on, Grace. What?"

"The Sanderton, that boutique hotel just down the road from us...they've opened a swanky new spa, and they're promoting it to the locals," Grace mumbled. "They've got *amazing* offers on here."

Saff grabbed the leaflet and read out loud, "'*The Sanderton is proud to introduce its new Haven Spa. Indulge yourself with the latest luxury treatments and state-of-the-art facilities for the ultimate pampering experience*'. Oh my God. What an absolute nightmare," she gasped. For once, I didn't think she was being overdramatic.

"We can't compete with this," Mum muttered, finding her voice again. "I mean, look on the back of the leaflet – it offers everything we do, and it has a pool, sauna and steam room as well. Which means they can do day pamper packages with lunch."

I felt sick and trembly too, but I reached for something positive to say. "It's not like we're the only beauty place in Totnes," I pointed out. "There's a big spa at The Royal Devon, but that's never bothered us."

"They're much further away," said Grace. "And they don't target locals – it's really just for hotel guests on package deals. These leaflets have been put round in the shops for local people to pick up. *Our customers.*"

"I don't even understand how they can offer these services for such low prices," Mum said. "I mean, look at this – a massage with free facial for £25. And this – free manicure when you book a pedicure."

Grace peered at the leaflet over my shoulder and raised her eyebrows. "Those offers are loss leaders, to get people in the door," she told us. "They won't make money on them, but they hope clients will spend on products, and book in for extras and other treatments at higher prices. It's like the supermarket selling beans for 10p and then once you're in there you buy other full-price stuff. The Sanderton's part of a chain. Head office is probably paying for this."

Hearing that, it felt like my stomach had dropped into my shoes. "But how are small businesses like us supposed to compete against that?" I stuttered.

"We aren't," Grace said flatly.

I really thought I was going to throw up then. We'd just got the business going, and now it looked like we had a huge battle on our hands. We were on target to make our next rent payment, but we still had a long way to go. What if business was badly affected by the new spa? How would we pay Mr. Vulmer then?

We all sat round the table, feeling sick and shocked, the coffee going cold and all thoughts of croissants forgotten. The Haven Spa opened on Monday morning and it felt like we were waiting for a hurricane to hit, to find out how bad the damage to our business would be.

We still had to deep-clean the treatment rooms after that, and look at what stock needed to be made or ordered in, but there was no more laughing and joking. We dragged around miserably, and I hardly felt like I had the energy to do anything. Grace was taking her frustration out on the floor, which was lucky because it needed a good scrub, but Saff seemed to have stopped completely, and was just leaning on the reception desk staring at the stock lists.

It was Mum who pulled us together in the end. "Come on, let's finish up and get out of here," she said. "There's no point hanging around moping. Let's walk up to the supermarket and get the ingredients to cook a big roast. We haven't had one since we've been here, and I really fancy it now autumn's in the air."

"Mum, we can't *cook* our way out of this crisis," said Grace flatly.

"I know that," said Mum, giving her a nudge, "but I want us to do something together. And a decent meal always makes things seem a bit better. Come on, Gracie, we can have beef. With Yorkshires…"

Grace's favourite.

"Fine," said my sister, "but only if there's pudding as well."

So, by half two, after lots of shopping and chopping and peeling and searing and basting and boiling and, erm, whatever it is you do to cook Yorkshire puds, we all sat down around the formica-topped table and had our first roast dinner on it.

About halfway through, as I was reaching for

more carrots, I noticed that the darkness I'd fel earlier had lifted a little. And perhaps the roast dinner had worked a bit of magic, because when the problem of the Haven Spa came into my mind (for about the hundredth time) instead of just feeling sick and blank and shuddery, I saw a little shoot of hope. "You know, we can't beat them on price," I said, "but we could create our *own* offer, and put leaflets in all the shops too."

"Good thinking," said Mum. "We can't just roll over and let them take our business."

"No way!" Saff agreed.

"We need to think of something that doesn't cost us too much, though, or we'll actually start *losing* money," Grace warned.

"How about a free manicure with every massage or other body treatment?" I suggested. "The cost is mainly Saff's time, isn't it?"

"Yes," said Grace. "The nail polish and other bits don't cost much."

"I'm happy to do as many as you can book in," said Saff eagerly.

"I'll sort out the leaflet," I said. "We can do it at school tomorrow. Summer can help and I'm sure Mr. Mac will let us use the Media Lab if we explain what it's for."

"Then we'll hit the streets and put them *everywhere*!" cried Saff. "We'll let that new spa know who they're dealing with! No one messes with the Green girls!"

"It's not about us being *against* them. We're simply promoting our business in a professional manner, that's all," said Mum, but she did give Saff a proud smile.

We'd bought a chocolate cheesecake too, which Mum produced from the fridge with a flourish as we were clearing the lunch plates away. It was delicious, and we even had our traditional argument about who'd got the biggest bit, which made it feel like Sundays used to in our lovely house in Ealing.

Well, almost.

I supposed that nothing would ever be exactly the same again, not with Dad gone. But perhaps we'd make some new traditions of our own, like Saff nicking a bit of Grace's cheesecake when she wasn't looking and then Grace chasing her round the table.

As we cleared up afterwards, Saff mentioned possibly going into town later to meet Emily, but Mum went all parenty on her. "No one's going out this evening," she shrilled. "It's the first day of school tomorrow, or college in your case, Saff, and I want you to have an early night. And, by the way, we're all going for an afternoon walk now, together, as a family, in the fresh air."

"You're joking!" Saff cried.

But Mum wasn't, and amazingly, Saff somehow ended up walking down a country road and then the track along the back fields with us. And even more amazingly, she managed to do the whole thing without moaning and I can officially report that she can now walk past a sheep without having a fit of terror and saying it's looking at her strangely and is about to charge! (Do sheep even *do* that?!)

Saff stayed in with us that night too, and we all squashed up on the revolting brown sofa with steaming mugs of tea cupped in our hands and watched our fave programme, *Embarrassing Bodies*, on the tiny telly.

A few minutes in, Mum sighed and said, "Oh, you're all leaving me tomorrow and doing your own thing – Rainbow Beauty won't be the same."

"Mum, we're going to school, not Timbuktu!" Grace cried. "We'll be back in the afternoons to help out. And all day Saturday."

"And I'll be with you on Tuesdays, for my work-placement day," Saff reminded her.

Mum smiled. "I know. It just feels strange, that's all. It's been me and my girls for the whole summer."

She put her arms round Saff and I, and I pulled
Grace in too, and we had a sort of sitting-sideways
hug. Amazingly, no one got scalded by hot tea.

"OMG, is that what I think it is?!" Saff gasped a
few seconds later. "That poor, poor man!"

We all peered at the weeny, rubbish screen for a
moment, then made out what the embarrassing bit
actually *was* and all screeched and turned away,
covering our eyes. And then I found myself thinking
that if we'd had a huge telly, and a big armchair each,
it wouldn't have been half so much fun.

Chapter Four

I spent ages getting ready for school on Monday morning, even by Saff's standards. I used our Rainbow Beauty Luscious Lavender Shower Gel for relaxation, but not even a truckload of lavender would have calmed me down right then because I was SO EXCITED that I'd be seeing Marco, my BOYFRIEND, every day – yippee! And I felt much better about the new spa opening now that we'd come up with a plan to tackle it head-on.

My uniform was Summer's old one that she'd passed on to me, so of course it was already pretty cool, but I jazzed it up even more by rolling up the skirt, knotting my tie loosely with pearl necklaces draped around it, and putting on loads of bracelets and hairslides. *And* my usual ton of black and grey eye make-up, of course.

Mum nearly had a heart attack when I walked out of the bathroom. "You look more done up than you did on Saturday night!" she cried. "Abbie, you're not going on a date, you know! I hope you're not going to be distracted by Marco at school. It's about getting a good education."

I grinned. "I promise I'll be the perfect student," I said. As I caught Saff's eye, she winked at me.

"I saw that!" Mum cried. (Of course she did – she never misses anything.) "I mean it, Abbie. School's not a lurve palace."

"A *lurve palace?*" I repeated, shuddering with horror. "Mum, where on earth did you get *that* from?"

"No, school is not a *lurve palace*, Abigail," said Saff, all primly, and Mum looked smug about her swapping sides, until she added, "School is a catwalk."

Mum groaned.

"And so is college," Saff added. "How do I look?"

"Great. Obviously. As ever," I said, with a sigh. It's not easy having stunning Saff for a sister and natural beauty Summer for a best friend. It's lucky I'm fairly confident, that's all I can say. Otherwise I'd just want to hide in the loos all the time with a bag over my head.

And then it got even worse, because Grace came out looking so jaw-dropping, we hardly recognized her.

She'd jazzed up her uniform, and she must have plaited her hair when it was wet the night before because it fell in beautiful glossy waves over her shoulders.

"Wow, Grace!" I gasped.

"Look out, Year 11!" cried Saff.

The sweep of black eyeliner and mascara made Grace's eyes look big and bright, and I was sure Mum would veto the gothy dark plum lipstick she'd paired with it, but she didn't say anything except, "My goodness, darling, you look lovely."

Grace allowed herself the tiniest smile. "Just because I've put on a bit of lippy doesn't mean I haven't got a brain," she announced.

"No one's saying it does, love," said Mum.

Then Grace peered at Saff, and the smallest frown flickered over her face.

"What?" Saff demanded.

"Oh, nothing," said Grace innocently, reaching for her bag.

"No, come on, what?" Saff cried.

Grace sighed. "Are you really wearing that top?" she said, with a cheeky grin. "It's just…it makes you look sort of mushroomy."

Yes, you read that right. She said that to Saff. As in, Ultimate Style Queen Saff.

"Mushroomy?" Saff repeated. "What does that even *mean*?"

But Grace just called out, "Come on, slowcoaches!", nicked the last bit of toast from Saff's plate and flounced off down the hall.

Saff walked as far as her bus stop to Paignton with Grace and me, and then we carried on up the road to Cavendish High. We linked arms, walking in time like we always did. I'd swapped the foul brown loafers Mum had made me wear on my first day for black ballet pumps, fortunately, and Grace had somehow managed to sneak Saff's slouchy boots past Mum, who'd have had a fit if she'd noticed her wearing them.

Things couldn't have been more different from when we'd arrived on our first day, a few months back. Now, instead of both being terrified about not knowing a single person, Grace and I were saying "hi" to people, and calling out and waving as soon as we walked through the gates. Grace spotted her friends Maisy and Aran near the canteen door and headed off to them. (I noticed Aran's jaw drop too, when he saw her new look!)

Then I spotted Marco, getting off his mum's motorbike and stowing his helmet. Sienna waved to me and I waved back, remembering how I'd panicked and thought she was Marco's girlfriend when I'd first seen her drop him off like that. She's lovely – really young and sparky. I didn't know what his dad was like because I'd never met him. From what Marco had said, Luke didn't have much to do with them, he just turned up sometimes and then disappeared off again.

As Sienna roared off and Marco slouched through the gates, what I actually wanted to do was that running-up-to-him thing with my arms out, like when people run through a meadow towards each other (does that ever really happen?!). But I forced myself to walk normally, even though my legs felt really weird, like I'd forgotten how. When I reached him, I didn't know whether to kiss him, hug him or what. I *didn't* want to look like a mental possessive person and be all over him, but on the other hand I *did* want anyone NOT yet aware via the gossip vine that we were together to get the message.

To be honest, what I *actually* wanted to do was make a giant placard with MARCO IS MY BOYFRIEND written on it, and carry it round – but

I'd definitely have looked a bit weird then. My brain was still whirring, trying to work out what to do next, when he gave me his big, gorgeous, lazy grin, said, "Hey, Abs", slung his arm round my shoulders and carried on walking. There. That's it. Perfect. Why can't *I* think of cool stuff like that?

The bell went and as we walked into class, just about everyone we saw said something about the cafe gig and how good it was. A really shallow bit of me was just LOVING walking down the corridor with the coolest guy in the year, who was my BOYFRIEND (oh, sorry, couldn't help mentioning that again!) but mostly I was just so proud of Marco. The gig *had* been great, and he told me they were getting loads of hits on their site, and tons of good comments and photos posted on Facebook. Obviously I had to check out the pics on Summer's phone before registration, and they really caught the warm, fun, tea-lighted atmosphere.

Then Ben turned up, and I told them all about the new spa. Summer looked really gutted for me, and Ben and Marco didn't seem sure *what* to say. "Is there anything we can do?" Summer asked.

"I'm hoping you'll help me make some leaflets of our own," I told them. "We're doing a free manicure with every body treatment."

"Good idea," said Summer. "I've still got some Rainbow Beauty pictures saved on the computers in the Media Lab from stuff we've done before – we can use those to jazz it up."

I smiled at her. "That's great. Are you all around at lunchtime?" I asked. "I'm going to see if we can use the lab then."

Ben and Summer were free, but Marco said, "I've got band practice, but I can put leaflets in the shops in town after school, and stick them on billboards and trees and stuff." *Oh, I could kiss that boy,* I thought. And I nearly did. But just then, Mrs. Leavis walked into our form room. We were 10L now, and as well as being our new form teacher, she took us for Geography and she was really nice. The first thing she talked about when she'd done the register was how it was all about GCSEs now. She kept mentioning building blocks and stepping stones and other ways of saying that this year is very, very important, even though we're not doing most of our actual exams until Year 11. I thought it was just Mrs. Leavis, because she's our form teacher, but everywhere we went all day we got the same talk.

When I went to the staffroom at break to ask Mr. Mac about using the Media Lab, he didn't hesitate to sign passes for me, Ben and Summer to be in there at lunchtime. He even said I could just pay cost price for the leaflets, so it worked out far cheaper than using a print shop.

So, as soon as the bell went after French, us three grabbed sandwiches from the canteen and headed over there. We designed the leaflets, then printed out batches on massive A3 sheets of glossy paper on the colour printer.

As we worked, I noticed that any awkwardness between Summer and Ben seemed to have completely melted away. Ben was happy because he got the total boy-job of chopping the A3 sheets into individual leaflets on the giant razor-sharp guillotine (Mr. Mac was in there doing some prep by that time, so he got it out of the store cupboard for us) and Summer and I got massively girly with the design and made Rainbow Beauty look like heaven on earth.

I felt so much better after we'd actually *done* something to counteract the new spa that I got really giggly and silly and completely embarrassed myself in Maths, thanks to my uncontrollable mouth. When Mrs. Croft announced that we'd be starting our preparation for our first piece of GCSE coursework straight away I found myself going "YEEEESSS!" very loudly, and everyone laughed. CRINGE! – I'd only meant to whisper it to Summer to be funny, but

I was so excited and happy about all the Headrush stuff and the me-and-Marco-ness in general, it came out at about a gazillion decibels, with an added air punch.

"I'm glad you're so excited about it, Miss Green," said Mrs. Croft, and then obviously I had to pretend I *was* so I didn't get told off, which made me CRINGE even more. All I can say is thank God Marco's in the top group (which I am so NOT, obviously!), so he wasn't there to witness my utter cringe-aciousness!

Us four were all together for English, though. It's one of my fave subjects and I'm really into it usually, but seeing Marco again after precisely forty-six minutes apart was so exciting that we ended up doing this flirty, whispery, note-passing thing and in the end Mr. King sighed and said, "Abbie and Marco, let me put it like this and maybe you'll pay more attention. So Marco, imagine Abbie is Juliet, and you're Romeo, and you're madly in love with each other, but your families want to keep you apart and you're gutted… What would you do about it?"

"Erm, I, well, we…" Marco mumbled.

Everyone cracked up, even me, as he went bright red and then got very interested in taking down the notes from the board.

While all this was going on, Summer and Ben, who were sitting opposite us, were chatting through stuff together before writing anything down. Their hands brushed as Summer opened her notebook and she quickly pulled hers away. Only *I* saw her looking a bit flustered. Ben either pretended not to notice or, probably, being a boy, he actually *didn't* notice. I couldn't help wondering, though – was she *really* over him? Maybe the awkwardness I'd spotted between them wasn't about what happened at the beach party after all. Maybe it was because she still liked him. I thought about asking her outright, but then I decided to just wait and see what happened. After the beach-party disaster, I was sure the last thing she needed was me trying to matchmake, even if she *did* still like Ben.

I gave most of the leaflets to Marco at last break (plus the kiss he hadn't got at registration time!) and Summer and Ben took a big bunch to put up round where they lived.

On the walk home, Grace and I stuck leaflets on every lamp post and tree (luckily, loads of drawing pins were left on them from previous posters) and in every letter box and shop window that we could find. By the time we arrived back at Rainbow Beauty, I was on a complete high. I'd convinced myself that we'd made the new spa out to be much more of a threat than it really was, and that with our clever bit of marketing we'd keep our customers coming to us.

When we showed Mum and Saff the leaflets, they were really impressed too, and Saff took a bunch to give out at her college in the morning. She was so excited about her first day, and bubbling over with chat about her tutors and the other girls (and the couple of boys) on her course, and what they learned, it lifted us all even more. "I'm glad I'm here to help you tomorrow," she said to Mum. "With such an enticing new offer, and leaflets everywhere, I'm sure the phone will be ringing off the hook from first thing in the morning."

I grinned at her. I was sure it would be too.

On Tuesday after school, Marco, Summer and Ben walked back to Rainbow Beauty with me. The boys were on their way into town and Summer was going to give me, Mum and my sisters a hand putting our Rainbow range together. And, of course, we were all keen to find out if the response to our leaflets had been as good as we'd hoped.

Mum met us at the door, beaming. "We've had seven bookings for the offer already," she told us. "I just wanted to thank you all for getting those leaflets done, and for all the legwork putting them up and giving them out."

"You're welcome, Mrs. Green," said Ben (SUCH perfect son-in-law material, that boy).

Marco shrugged and said, "No worries."

"We can stay and help too, if you like," Ben said to me, when Mum had gone back inside.

"Will I have to wear a hairnet again?" asked Marco, wrinkling up his nose.

I gave him a wicked grin. "Much as I'd enjoy seeing that, we're not making huge amounts or anything, just a couple of samples of each to send up to Dad. The main thing we need to do is get the colours right and decide on the final packaging for each one."

"You mean it's going to be a lot of girly stuff with ribbons and going 'Oooooh, smell this one. It's divine!'?" asked Ben.

"Yeah, *very* girly," I said. "And no heavy lifting involved."

"In that case, shall we give it a miss and go for that burger?" Marco asked Ben. He gave me his gorgeous smile. "You don't mind, do you?"

"Of course not," I said. "I was worried that you'd be off with me because I couldn't come out."

"No way," he insisted. "I know how important your business is."

"Who are you and what have you done with my vain, selfish mate Marco?" Summer cried, with a teasing look on her face. To prove he was still the same, he called her a cheeky cow. Then I gave him the longest hug I could get away with without looking like a total nutter, and the boys headed off.

Summer and I helped Mum finish up at Rainbow Beauty, and then we went upstairs with her, where we found my sisters cleaning down the kitchen and getting everything ready. They greeted Summer with big hugs and we scrubbed and aproned and hairnetted ourselves with mucho giggling.

Then Mum, Saff and Grace started adjusting the colours on our chosen products, and Summer and I got to work creating our new blueberry body butter. Because I hadn't made any before, and I didn't have a recipe to follow, it was a bit trial and error. We made a nice base of cocoa and shea butter and then added the blueberry oil. While it's great for dry skin, it doesn't have a smell, so we fiddled around with the blueberry fragrance oil that had arrived in the post that morning from our supplier, until we had something that smelled nice, but wasn't overpowering. The blue camomile mixed with alkanet gave us quite a good indigo colour in the end.

As we worked, Summer said, "Hey, I've been trying to think about how else you can advertise yourselves, to help you compete against this new spa, and I've had a thought. Instead of just helping out at the Autumn Fayre, you could have your own Rainbow Beauty stall."

"That sounds like a great idea," said Mum eagerly, overhearing. "You could do loads more of the leaflets, Abbie, and give them out. And if you take some products to sell, we could give, say, 20% of the profits to the charity. Oh, I hope that's enough? I wish it could be more, but—"

"Mum, with our slim profit margins that's really generous as it is," Grace cut in.

Summer smiled. "That would be amazing," she assured her.

"What if we could get the ingredients to make something for free…" I said, thinking aloud. "Then we could create a product especially for the Fayre and give *all* the money to charity."

"That's a great idea, Abbie," said Mum. "But where are we going to get free ingredients from?"

"I bet I can persuade our greengrocer to donate some stuff," said Summer. "You know, Tom, who let us do that photo shoot in his shop? He's always given a big fruit and veg box for the raffle, so I'm sure he won't mind."

"Great!" I cried. "How about having a theme? Like blueberries? Everyone likes those!"

"Oh, we could do fresh blueberry smoothies in that case," said Saff, "if we get a free box of bananas thrown in."

"And Blueberry Burst Fresh Face Masks," Grace suggested. "You could whizz them up right in front of people to create a bit of theatre, too."

Saff grimaced. "You'd have to take both blenders! No one wants face mask in their smoothie!"

"Obviously!" Grace tutted. "I'm not an idiot, you know!"

"Alright! Keep your knickers on!" snapped Saff.

"Great idea," said Mum quickly, before my sisters could blow it up into a full-scale row. "We can certainly donate the other ingredients for those, like the almond oil and so on."

"That would be fab," said Summer. "And hey, I know, we can sell Blueberry Wishes! We can get a load of sweet bags and put ten blueberries in each, then charge a pound a wish!"

She seemed surprised to find us all peering blankly at her. "Erm, what are you on about?" asked Saff.

Summer was peering back at us, looking equally confused. "Don't you know about Blueberry Wishes?" she cried. "I thought everyone did. Oh, well, maybe it's just my mad family. We've always done it, ever since we were little. You eat ten blueberries and make a wish, but you have to wish out loud or it won't come true. Come to think of it, it probably *was* just a way for Mum and Dad to get us to eat our fruit, but I swear it worked at the time. I got a bike for my birthday that year, just like I wanted."

Grace grinned. "The fact that your mum and dad heard you wish out loud for one must have helped!"

"Well, I think it's a great idea," I said. "Who are we to say how the mysterious powers of the universe work?"

I just said that to wind Grace up, and indeed she *did* mumble something about codswallop and try to swat me with a spatula, but then Mum said, "I might try it now, actually, though I'd have to eat about two hundred to wish away that new spa!"

"Oh, Mum, it'll be okay," I said.

She smiled. "I'm sure it will, love. Sorry, girls, I don't mean to put a downer on things. I'm just tired, that's all. It's been a busy day…thank goodness! And I've got my first client at half seven tomorrow morning.

She asked if she could come before work and I didn't want to say no. We need every booking we can get at the moment, especially now we've got competition."

"Why don't you go and have a bath?" Grace suggested. "We can get on with this. The Blueberry Body Butter is sorted, and we've just about adjusted the colours on the other products, too. We're only going to play around with packaging now. You can have a look at everything when you come out and give it your seal of approval."

Mum stifled a yawn. "I wouldn't usually leave you to it, but I think I'd better or I'll be hopeless at work tomorrow."

When she'd headed off to the bathroom, Summer, Saff, Grace and I tried out different packaging. It all had to be transparent, of course, to show the colours, but we had a big selection of sample bottles and jars that we'd got from our supplier to play around with when we'd first set up the business. We put the body butter in a lovely glass jar with an almost round base in the end, and we all agreed that it was the best choice.

"Wow, it suddenly looks really classy and expensive," Summer remarked.

"It'll have to," I said, "what with the prices Grace will want to charge the London boutiques for it!"

Grace took that as a compliment and smiled proudly.

"And we could create beautiful little vintage-y labels," Saff suggested, "to complete the look."

"And could we borrow your wish thing for the name, Summer?" I asked. "Blueberry Wishes Body Butter?"

Summer looked really pleased. "Yeah, sure," she said.

A while later, when we'd settled on the best fit of bottles and jars for the rainbow products and lined them all up in colour order on the table, Mum came out of the bathroom in her dressing gown, looking much better. "Oh, they look wonderful," she exclaimed.

"Glad you like them," I said.

"We just need to get the body butter tested, as it's a new product, and then that's everything done," said Grace. "Saff's going to pop it in to the cosmetic chemist in Paignton tomorrow before college."

"And if everything's okay with it, I should be able to pick up the certificate afterwards," Saff added, "so we'll have it ready to give to Dad with everything else when Abbie briefs him at the weekend."

"That's great," said Mum. "You girls really have got everything covered."

"Hey, I know, I could come and do nails at the Fayre," Saff offered. "I bet you'd make stacks of extra cash that way."

"I'm sorry, love, but I need you here," said Mum. "You'll have loads of manicure appointments, thanks to our offer. And, Grace, I'll need you out front to welcome people, and sell products once they've had their treatments, otherwise they tend to just leave without browsing."

"Oh, yeah, course," said Grace, and Saff gave a little nod too.

Summer's brother Jim beeped the horn of their Land Rover outside, so we said our goodbyes and had lots more hugs. (Ben's right – we *are* totally girly!)

Then we sat round the table and looked at our beautiful new rainbow of products. "The London shops will love these," Saff said excitedly. "And we'll have to think of ways to tell our local customers about them too – they *are* unique to us, after all. You can't just walk into *any old place* and buy them."

We all smiled, knowing that *any old place* actually meant the *brand-spanking-new place* down the road.

Mum smiled. "My clever, wonderful girls," she sighed.

Grace grinned. "I know that the new spa opening isn't great news, but I really think we've got it covered now," she said. "Between our promotion and the stall at the Autumn Fayre, I'm sure we've done enough to keep our customers, and hopefully get some new ones too. Things are going to be fine, I can just feel it. And of course, the London side of the business should be growing too, so soon we won't just be relying on income from Rainbow Beauty itself."

We looked at each other and smiled. If *Grace* thought things would be okay – cautious, careful Grace – well, then, surely they would be.

Chapter Five

On Wednesday when I got back from school, I was supposed to be doing my History homework. In fact, I'd accidentally let slip that it was due in on Friday and so Mum was insisting on it (I am quite famous in our family for leaving schoolworky things until the absolute last minute and then driving everyone mad by stressing out about them). Instead I slouched around Rainbow Beauty, looking for a job to do.

"You won't find anything that needs to be ordered, cleaned or sorted out down here," said Mum smugly, as she dried up the smoothie glasses, leaning on the door frame of the kitchenette. She'd had a steady stream of customers who'd seen our offer leaflets, and people were booking in for the next few days too, so she was looking very happy. "I've made sure everything's done, so you've no excuse not to go and get on with that homework."

It was just looking like I *would* really have to go upstairs and get on with it when I decided to see if her happy mood was happy enough to let me go and see Marco, just for a little while.

"No way," she said flatly, when I suggested it.

"But, Muuuum," I moaned, "I can't stop thinking about him. I mean, there is literally, probably *medically*, no actual room for History homework in my head right now! Once I've seen him, I'll be able to stop *thinking* about seeing him and concentrate on my work."

"But you've seen him all day!" Mum said, looking unconvinced.

"No, I haven't," I insisted. "Well, only for a tiny while, at first break. Apart from that I was far too busy Engaging Fully With My Education to give any time to my personal relationships. I do take my future very seriously, you know."

I leaped out of the way as Mum swatted at me with her tea towel. "Go on, then. But make sure you're back by seven and straight to work, or I'll ban you from seeing that boy!"

"Oh, that would be soooo romantic, like Romeo and Juliet!" I cried as I swanned over to the door. "Which I've been paying full attention to in English, you'll be pleased to know!"

"Cheeky madam! Seven, and not a second later!" Mum called, and I gave her an angelic smile and hurried out before she changed her mind.

I was going to text him first, but Saff had gone out with Emily and taken our shared mobile, so I decided to just turn up at his flat, and then try the rehearsal studio if he wasn't in.

My heart jumped as Marco's front door opened and I saw him standing there.

"Hey, Abs," he said, giving me his lazy smile, which was actually going a *tiny* bit towards grinning idiot.

I was doing *total* grinning idiot, of course, and it was a relief when he pulled me into a hug. I was just thinking about kissing him (well, of course I was) when his mum leaned out of the kitchen doorway. "Oh, Abbie!" she cried. "Come in, come in."

Marco wrinkled his nose at me. "Do you mind?" he asked.

"Course not," I insisted. I really liked Sienna – I

guess to Marco she was just his embarrassing mum, but to me she seemed more like a movie star or something.

As we walked past the living room, I glanced in and spotted Marco's guitar propped against the wall. Even the sight of his *stuff* gave me a happy glow inside, for goodness' sake.

In the kitchen, there were three places set for dinner. "Would you like to stay, love?" asked Sienna. "It's my famous chicken risotto."

"Oh, yes, please," I said, remembering that it was help-yourself-to-salad night at home. It smelled delicious and I realized that I hadn't eaten anything since that apple at last break. "But how did you know I was coming?" I asked, gesturing at the place settings.

Sienna smiled. "Oh, I didn't. It's for…"

"…my dad," Marco finished, just as Luke walked in.

I couldn't help staring at him. Luke, I mean. I'd seen an old photo, but even if I hadn't, I'd have known he was Marco's dad. He had the same piercing blue eyes, the same slow, lazy smile. He held out his hand and I stared at it for ages before coming to and realizing that I was supposed to shake it. "I'm Luke, nice to meet you," he said.

"I'm Abbie," I managed to stutter. My mind was racing. Marco hadn't mentioned anything about his dad at school that day. Had he just turned up out of the blue? Did Sienna mind? How did Marco feel about it?

"Oh, I guessed," Luke was saying. "Marco can't stop talking about you..."

Marco emerged from the fridge, where he'd been rummaging for the Parmesan. I grinned at him. "Oh, you can't, huh?" I teased.

He looked so cute standing there blushing, holding this massive wedge of cheese, that I wanted to leap over and wrap him up in my arms. But I didn't, obviously. Not in front of his mum. And dad. His mum and dad. Wow, that sounded weird.

Luke emptied a bag of rocket into a bowl and got some salad servers from a drawer, then pulled a few bottles of wine from the rack on the counter and looked at them before choosing one. I couldn't help thinking that Mum would kill Dad if he just started helping himself to this or that (she barely even let him have a *coffee* when he came to our flat), but Sienna acted like everything was normal. I guess it was, for her. The way Marco had explained it, his dad came and went like this.

"You didn't tell me he was coming," I said softly to Marco, as he poured orange juice for us two.

"I didn't know," he said. "I walked in after rehearsal and…" He motioned towards Luke.

"What, with no warning, nothing? Isn't your mum annoyed?"

Marco shrugged. "She's used to it."

At that moment, Luke came over to put the salad and the wine on the table then, so we couldn't talk about him any more. Next, Sienna put a huge pot of risotto in the middle and we all sat down to eat.

I thought it would be really awkward, trying to think of things to say, but Sienna mentioned Rainbow Beauty to Luke, and he asked me about it and soon I found myself telling him about the problems we were facing with the new spa on our doorstep, and how we'd come up with our own promotion to counter it.

I tried to stay on my guard, but when he said how much he admired us for starting our own business I couldn't help smiling, and he beamed back at me. "I'm sure that Haven Spa issue's just a blip," he added. "People like to try new things – but they'll soon find they prefer your personal service and home-made products."

"Absolutely," said Sienna. "No one can resist the kind of introductory offers they're making, but they can't possibly afford to keep that up. You'll soon be able to compete with them on an even footing again."

"I hope so," I said.

"And you can create more new offers all the time," added Marco. "We can help put posters up and stuff."

I smiled at him. "Thanks."

"That Avocado Body Butter I bought last time I was at your place was amazing," Sienna enthused. "You could give one away with each treatment."

"That's an idea," I said, giving her a smile. "And you're right, you all are. We probably shouldn't be too worried about it. After all, plenty of people are coming in because of our offer already."

By the time we got to the panna cotta (this yummy Italian set-mousse thing) I found myself liking Luke despite trying not to. Well, he was so like Marco, it would have been hard not to warm to him.

Then we started talking about the band, and Luke was really keen to hear all about their last gig at the cafe and all the website and Facebook and SoundCloud interest they'd had. "Next time you rehearse, I'd love to come and have a listen if that's okay," he said.

Marco looked at the table, but I didn't have to see his eyes to know there was hurt in them. I could feel it radiating from him. I knew he was remembering all the times Luke had promised to come to things, then not turned up, and all the times he'd seemed interested in him, then dropped him like a stone and gone off again. "We're not booked into the studio until Friday so you probably won't—" Marco mumbled.

"I'll be here," said Luke. He sighed. "Look, I know I haven't stuck around in the past, but it's different this time. I wanted to come down and be closer to you while I've got the chance. In a couple of years, you'll be all over the place doing who knows what, touring with your band, probably. You'll be way too busy to see your old man."

Marco glanced up at him, then had another good stare at his pudding. "Yeah, heard it before," he muttered.

"Seriously. I mean it this time," Luke insisted. "I've got somewhere nearby to stay, and another mate might have a job for me at a venue in Exeter, so I'm planning to stick around for as long as you're here…if that's okay?"

All three of us were looking at Marco then. He just shrugged and said, "Whatever."

Luke sighed. "I know it's hard to believe in me, son," he said. "But it's different this time. I'll prove that to you. You'll see."

Marco didn't say anything at all to that. I glanced

at Sienna, because it seemed like someone ought to be saying *something*, but she was concentrating very hard on her plate, being careful *not* to react. I was so glad when Marco ended the awkward silence by changing the subject.

After supper, I offered to help clear up, and Marco dragged his dad into the living room to play him some new song he couldn't *believe* he hadn't heard yet. ("Call yourself a muso?" he'd sneered.) As I cleared the table, I heard Marco talking about another new band.

"Oh yeah, they played at the club a few weeks back," said Luke.

"Wow, that's… I wish I'd seen them," Marco stuttered, clearly impressed. "Hey, I bet you haven't heard of these guys yet, though. They've just started trending but I've known about them for months…" And he put on another song.

"CHOON!" cried Luke, which I didn't know dads were allowed to say, but maybe Luke didn't count as a proper dad anyway.

"Luke's really nice," I said to Sienna as I stacked the plates up beside the sink. I glanced at her, still looking for a reaction to the news that he was staying. I wondered if she'd known that already, or whether it had been just as much of a surprise to her as to Marco.

"Yeah," she said, pulling on a pair of washing-up gloves and filling the sink, revealing nothing.

"It's nice that he's sticking around," I ventured.

"I'll believe it when I see it," Sienna mumbled. There. That was the reaction I'd been scared of. Huge great alarm bells started going off in my head.

"Oh, don't worry. Marco won't fall for it either," she assured me, seeing the look on my face. "It's just the way Luke is. He's all or nothing. And at the time, he really means it, about changing, and sticking around. But he'll go again. Marco knows that."

"Shouldn't you, like, *say* something?" I said. Yikes, I was only supposed to *think* that.

Sienna stopped the taps, glanced towards the door, then turned to me. She sighed. "Look, I can't keep them from each other," she said, in a low voice. "I wouldn't want to – they're father and son. And of course I really hope Luke keeps his promises this time."

She smiled at me and I managed a small smile back, while thinking, *So do I*.

"And it's great that Marco's got you," she added. "I was so pleased to hear you two had sorted things out. He's been so happy since you've been back together."

I couldn't help grinning then. "Me too," I said. I managed to shut my big mouth before it added,

I'm crazy about him. Whatever happens with Luke, I'll never let him down.

"Oh, I've got something for you," Sienna said when we'd finished the washing-up. She peeled off her pink rubber gloves and vanished down the hallway. A few minutes later, she came back with a gorgeous purple scarf with tassel ends. "I loved it so much that I couldn't resist getting it, but it's not my colour," she explained. "It makes me look like I've got the norovirus." She held it up to herself and pulled a face.

"No, it doesn't—" I began, but she waved my words away.

"Anyway, I thought it would really suit you," she said, "so here." She handed it to me.

"Wow, are you sure?" I asked. I put it on straight away and Sienna nodded approvingly.

"I knew it would look great," she said. "But then, you'd look good in a bin bag."

I really wanted to hug her, but I didn't quite (note to self: get more Italianly expressive!) so instead I ended up thanking her loads instead.

Sienna was going to make us all coffee to have in the living room, but I knew I really ought to be back by seven if Mum was going to let me out anywhere ever again.

I explained about my History homework and thanked her for dinner, and then told Marco I had to make a move. We did hug then, and do the Italian three-cheek-kissing thing. And I did the two-cheek-kissing thing with Luke (even though what I'd really wanted to do was the I'm-watching-you thing where you point to your eyes and then their eyes while pulling a Face of Suspicion).

Me and Marco went into the hallway. "I'll walk you home," he said, reaching for his jacket from the pegs by the door.

"No, I'm fine, really – you stay with your dad," I insisted. "Make the most of him while…" I stopped myself, but it was too late. I could tell from Marco's frown that he was filling in the rest of that sentence.

"You don't think he'll stick around, do you?" he asked.

I didn't know what to say. What *could* I say? "Well, it's just, from what it sounds like, this is kind of what he does…" I mumbled, going bright red.

"It's okay," said Marco, squeezing my hand. "I'm not offended or anything. I don't think he'll stay either. But he says he wants to prove that he's changed. He's never said that before. So I guess we'll see."

"Yeah, I guess," I said.

"I mean, you gave your dad another chance, didn't you? Even after everything that happened?"

I shrugged. "Yeah. I suppose so."

"Well, then, it's the same," said Marco.

I smiled. "Sure it is," I said.

I gave Marco an extra big hug, and we had a kiss, but not a snog-type one, because his mum and dad (that still sounded strange) were only about five metres away after all. It did *almost* turn into a snog-type one, but then I was sure one of them would appear any minute, so I managed to use all my willpower to pull myself away from him. Then we couldn't resist hugging again, and having a kiss, and then nearly a snog-type one, and the whole thing happened about five times before I finally managed to get myself out of the door.

As I strode down the street, I found myself turning it all over in my head.

With my own dad I'd decided to try and move forward and not let the past get in the way of the present. And I'd persuaded Grace to do that too. And Saff. So why was I being so hard on Luke? Why didn't Marco deserve that fresh start? And why didn't Luke deserve another chance? *Because he's had so many chances already*, I heard myself think. *And how many chances is too many? When do you walk away? And when it's someone as close as a dad, do you ever?*

In Media class on Thursday, Summer and I were using the opportunity to make posters for my stall at the Autumn Fayre. Strictly speaking, we were supposed to be inventing a product and each using different methods to promote it. We had seen our chance and put ourselves down to do a live event as our type of promotion. Of course, I'd created the blueberry face mask a while ago, but when I'd asked Mr. Mac if we could still use it, he'd let us because the event was for charity. I'd made a few pots of it the evening before, after finishing my History homework (finally, yippeeeee!) and brought them in to take photos.

Jess and Bex from netball were doing a web page for the sports support bandage they'd created, and Josh and Alex were working on a Facebook campaign for some kind of secret-recipe sauce they were claiming would become as big as Reggae Reggae Sauce (once they'd been on *Dragons' Den* and got the investment money of course). Raven and Selima were working on a promotional video for their mini-composters, and Jake and Max had gone off to film kids using their double yo-yo around the school.

Ben and Marco were…well, let's just say their product was still in development, so right at that moment they didn't have anything *to* promote. While everyone else was busy working on the computers along the side wall, or spreading artwork out on the big table, or running things off on the massive colour printer, the boys were being annoying and distracting me and Summer.

"Oh, come on, Abs. *Please* help us," Ben begged. "You always have loads of ideas and we've got literally zilchio."

"I've *had* an idea!" Marco protested. "You just won't do it, that's all."

"That's because it's rubbish!" Ben countered.

"What was it?" Summer asked Marco. "Come on, you can tell us. Ben's opinion isn't the be-all and end-all. You might have come up with the next big thing."

Ben pulled a face at her and she gave him two fingers.

"Okay," said Marco, giving Ben a smug look and shuffling his chair closer to us at the computer. "You know food, right?"

Summer and I looked at each other and smirked. "Yeah, we are aware of food," she said.

Marco ignored that. "Well, wouldn't it be good if you could have your favourite meals without doing any cooking?"

I wrinkled my nose at him. "Isn't that just called getting a takeaway?" I asked.

Marco sighed. "No, I mean, in a way that's easy and cheap and you don't have to wait for? So, I'm thinking, cereal, yeah? Why does it just have to be *cereal* flavour? People eat it as a snack all day, and after a night out and stuff. So how about doing kebab flavour? Or fish and chips? You could even have a roast-dinner one. You know, little different-coloured bits in the shape of roasties and beef and carrots."

"I think what you're describing is cat food," I smirked.

"See?" said Ben, rolling his eyes. "This is why you've got to help us!"

Marco elbowed him and he almost fell off his chair.

"Sorry, but the cereal thing *is* awful," said Summer.

"Totally yuck!" I added.

"I've thought of a product *you* definitely need, though," said Summer, grinning at Ben. "Self-washing socks!"

"Yeah, yeah!" cried Marco. "Even better, socks

that have a built-in air freshener that activates when you move! Abs, you could invent that. It could be aromatherapy," he added, laughing.

Ben called him a word I can't really write down here, and tried to pull his chair out from under him. "Aromatherapy socks," he said. "I know you were joking, but there's something in that. This could make our fortune, mate. We need a tag line, though."

"Sweet Feet," I said, just off the top of my head.

"Cheers, Abs," said Ben, scribbling it down.

"Now we've done your work for you, could you let us get on with ours, do you think?" asked Summer, raising her eyebrows and giving Ben a cheeky grin.

"Be my guest," he said, smiling back. They didn't stop looking at each other for ages and somewhere in the back of my brain, cogs were whirring, and thoughts were forming, and wonderings, like the ones I'd wondered in English, were being wondered.

But I didn't have time to focus on them, because Summer had brought our draft poster over from the printer and was holding it in front of my face. "Boooo-ring!" she declared.

I had to admit I could see what she meant. We'd uploaded the photos she'd taken of the face-mask pots, but even half-open to show the lovely blue mixture inside and dressed up with a few blueberries, the poster still didn't look very exciting. We fiddled with the fonts and text size, and Mr. Mac suggested changing the background colour, which we tried, but that didn't improve it very much either.

That was when Summer looked at me and did another of her cheeky smiles. "It would be more eye-catching if someone actually *wore* the face mask," she said. She nudged me and glanced towards the boys. I grinned too – having a boy rather than a girl on the posters would be even *more* eye-catching, plus it was a great chance to wind them up.

Summer wandered over to the big table where the socks campaign was taking shape, and informed Marco that he was going to be the new face of Blueberry Wishes Face Mask.

He smirked, obviously not taking her seriously. "Why me? What about you two?"

"I'll be taking the photos and Abbie's too busy designing," said Summer.

"Yeah, I'm too busy designing," I called, from the computers, swooshing the mouse around and peering at the screen.

"Ben'll do it. Won't you, mate?" said Marco. "*I* can't. I'm probably, like, allergic to it."

"It's all natural ingredients," I told him, "so you shouldn't be."

"Oh, come on. It's for charity," said Summer. "You look more the sort to use a face mask than Ben."

"Oh, cheers!" cried Marco.

Ben looked smug. "Are you saying I'm the rugged, manly type?" he said to Summer.

"She's saying you look like a tramp, mate," I heard Marco reply. But I wasn't looking at him. I was watching my best friend. She'd gone all red and stuttery when Ben had said the *rugged-manly* thing, and she was taking a big interest in her shoes. They were *quite* interesting – I mean, they were cool DMs with little flowers painted on and one yellow and one red ribbon for laces – but they weren't *that* interesting.

"No, I just meant that Marco's got a more urban look than you and—" Summer began, then trailed off into embarrassed mumbling.

Ben was actually blushing beetroot by then, and also looking like he wanted his plastic chair to magically eject him out through the ceiling. What if Summer still liked him (hence the red-and-stutteriness) and what if he liked her now too (hence the beetroot-blushing)? (Look at me, saying "hence"! See, I'd SO been listening in English!) Well, that would be just *perfect*, wouldn't it?

To check out my theory in a scientific way, I needed more evidence, so I smiled sweetly and said, "I've changed my mind. You're doing the face-mask poster, Ben. No arguing. Summer, you get it on him while I finish this."

Well, they both looked horrified. But they didn't argue. And there was a lot of awkward blushing and mumbling and general embarrassment as Summer applied the gloopy purple mask to his face.

Actually, I'm not sure what that proved. Perhaps Ben just felt like an idiot (everyone had cheered and done a big round of applause as she was dolloping it on him, which can't have helped). But maybe there was more to it than that. If there was, I was determined to find out for definite.

When the pictures were done, Ben went to wash the face mask off (while grumbling about annoying girls and how we *so* owed him an iced bun as compensation at last break), and Summer came and sat down next to me to load them up onto the computer. I didn't say anything about Ben to her, though. I was too terrified about getting it wrong, like I did before the beach party, and somehow messing up our group. I'd need to be totally sure they liked each other before I said anything.

* * *

I found myself watching Ben and Summer on Friday too — I didn't realize I was, but when they were sharing a textbook in Geography, Summer suddenly did that goggly eyes thing at me, as if to say, *What are you staring at?*

"Sorry, I'm miles away," I whispered. "Just thinking about seeing Dad tomorrow."

She looked all concerned then and asked me if I was feeling okay about that, and I felt really bad for fibbing. I realized when she asked the question that actually I was just mainly looking forward to seeing him, and I only had a tiny bit of the stomach-churning, *how-dare-you-wreck-our-family* type feeling that I used to get all the time, whenever I even *thought* of him.

I hoped Grace and Saff would be alright too. Well, I mean, they'd both sorted out their differences with him and things were all okay on the phone, so there was no reason why they wouldn't be. In a strange, non-logical way, I wished Mum could come too, so we could all be together again, and get along just like we used to. I guess what I really wanted to do was turn back time, to when we were in our cosy, happy house in Ealing, laughing and teasing and bustling about and talking non-stop.

But I'd accepted that we could never go back — and at least now we had some way of going forwards.

Mum, Grace, Saff and I had Rainbow Beauty, new friends, the flat and each other. My sisters and I had Dad back in our lives. It wasn't perfect, but it was our life now, and I was really beginning to love it.

Chapter Six

On Saturday afternoon, Dad met Saff, Grace and me at Victoria Coach Station in London and we all had massive hugs (and Dad had a couple of tears, which Saff didn't notice and Grace and I pretended not to see).

"Nice look, Dad!" said Saff approvingly, and I remembered that only Grace and I had seen him go back to being suited and booted and smelling of aftershave like he used to.

We were expecting to head back to his flat – well, bedsit – but he had a surprise for us. Massimo, the owner of a gorgeous vintage-style beauty shop called Beau, had invited us in to present the new range at two o'clock. We'd pitched to him before when we were selling our Beauty and the Beach range, and he'd ordered loads, so Saff and I were really excited.

But Grace looked horrified. "Dad, it's already twelve," she gasped, "and we haven't even shown you the new products or gone through the pricing or anything!"

"Well, we'd better get cracking then," said Dad, with a grin.

So we found an Italian cafe just down from the coach station and us three ordered paninis while Dad got a massive plate of bolognese. Grace made him wear a load of paper napkins tucked into his collar in case he got any down his shirt right before the pitch. I couldn't help smiling, watching her fuss over him – I knew just how much courage it had taken her to give him another chance.

We walked into Beau at two on the dot and were greeted like old friends by Massimo himself, with the three-kisses-on-the-cheek thing that Marco's mum does. He'd made us coffee in a posh cafetière and there were long, thin biscotti with pistachios and orange peel. He told us how well the Beauty and the Beach range had gone down with his customers, and then we pitched the Rainbow range to him. He loved the concept and was especially keen on the Red Spicy Delight Bubble Bath and the Blue Massage Oil Blend. He took ten each of those and eight of everything else, as well as five of the gift packs.

Saff's eyes were popping out – she hadn't pitched with us before, so she was only used to seeing people buy one or two products at a time. Grace and Dad looked quietly pleased. Over lunch they'd agreed that sixty orders would be brilliant. Luckily I managed to control myself from going "Yes!" and punching the air or doing a happy dance or anything.

After that, Massimo spent time chatting with us and showing us some of the other new products he'd got in recently from different suppliers. "Florals mixed with citrus are trending right now," he told us. "Here, smell this."

"Citrus – see?" said Saff smugly to Grace, as he handed us all little bottles of hand cream.

I was soon lost in the heady scents of orange, jasmine and… "Is that rose?" I asked, breathing in the delicious scent.

"Yes," said Massimo, looking impressed. "They're free samples. Take them if you like."

Then he showed us a new men's range he'd ordered. "It's good quality," he said, "but I don't like their scrub as much as yours." (He'd displayed our Zingy Lime and Ginger Sea Salt Body Scrub in the men's section as well as the women's and now it was all sold out.)

That was when I happened to glance at Grace and found her doing a goggly eyes thing at me. After a few seconds, I caught on to what she was getting at. "Oh, I'm sure we can make you some more, no problem," I told him.

"That would be fabulous," said Massimo. "Put me down for ten."

"Thank you. We really appreciate your support," Dad said.

"It's a great product," said Massimo. "And it's a pleasure for me to encourage new talents like Abbie. Young people like her are the future of the beauty business."

Erm, the FUTURE of the BEAUTY BUSINESS? Me? OMG, with bells on. It really hit me then – I'd started off creating a few products at the kitchen table to try and cheer up Mum and my sisters, and now I was standing here selling them to one of the smartest beauty shops in London. I stared at a wall display of moisturizers and tried to act normal and not have a total hysterical freak-out.

"Do men spend a *lot* on tarting themselves up

then?" I heard Saff asking, when I came round from my OMG moment.

"On *grooming*, yes," Massimo said, giving her an amused smile.

"That's something we should look into for the future," said Grace thoughtfully. "We could do a whole men's range."

"Well, it's probably just in London," said Saff. "I bet some of the hippy blokes down where we live don't even use *soap*!"

"Oh, you'd be surprised," said Massimo. "Male grooming is big everywhere now."

"Maybe we could market some of our products as unisex and sell to men too..." said Grace, thinking aloud.

"You remind me of myself at your age," Massimo told her, "always looking for the next business opportunity."

"And me. Like father, like daughter," said Dad proudly.

While Grace was blushing about a zillion degrees but trying to look cool about the compliments, Massimo said, "I'm creating an autumn display themed around berries or spices for the men's window, and if you can provide something along those lines, I'll include it. I really like your Red Spicy

Delight Bubble Bath, but it's a bit too sweet for men, and they don't really buy bath products, as such."

We all gaped at each other. Being asked to make a bespoke product – what a massive opportunity! Then I realized that Dad and my sisters were staring at me, not just to go "Wow!", but because they were waiting for me to come up with something on the spot.

I know a lot of things my mouth comes out with on its own are embarrassing, but for a change it said something sensible, i.e., "We could make it into a shower gel instead." As Massimo nodded approvingly I found myself thinking of Marco's spicy, woody smell. "And, erm, we could keep the frankincense and ginger as they're the deeper notes from the Red bubble bath you like, but swap the sandalwood for cedarwood, and bring in some musk and cinnamon." I managed to stop myself from adding, *Which is how my BOYFRIEND smells.*

Massimo grinned. "I wouldn't have thought of that combination, but it sounds divine. If you do develop something, send me a sample and we'll go from there."

"Okay, great...thanks," I stuttered.

Massimo had to head off to a meeting then, so when the orders were written up and the deposit paid, we said our goodbyes and stepped out into the street, walking on air.

"That was amazing!" cried Saff. "He really loved the products, and our brand, and *us*!"

"Great, isn't it?" said Dad. "When it goes well, sales is the best job in the world! And he was right, you *are* all really talented."

"Well, if you don't mind, I'm off to be really talented somewhere else," said Saff, pulling a little mirror from her bag to check her hair and make-up. "I'm meeting Sabrina on Kensington High Street and then we're having dinner out with the rest of the Arts Ed lot, so don't cook anything for me." She slicked on some more lip gloss. "See you guys about nine-ish?"

"Sure," I said, giving her a big hug. "Have fun."

"Watch your bag on the Tube," said Grace gravely. "This *is* London."

"Yes, where I *have* lived for most of my life," Saff told her, pulling a face.

Me and Grace were going straight back to Dad's with him. I had thought about meeting Em and Zo that afternoon but I hadn't called them in the end. Last time I'd seen them we hadn't gelled like we used to, and I'd found myself wishing the time away. It was like our lives had gone in different directions.

They weren't the same, or rather, *they* were – but I wasn't.

Luckily Emily had loaned Saff her old phone for the weekend, so Dad told Saff to text him when she got off the Tube and he'd walk up and meet her at the station. Then we all saw her onto the right bus and waved her off.

When we got back to Dad's place, I was impressed to see that it was still looking as good as Saff and me had left it after our cleaning spree. Mum had given me the pay-as-you-go phone to bring, and I rummaged in my bag for it. I burst into a huge grin when I saw that there was a text from Marco. *Look in the side pocket of your bag*, it read, in texty language. So I did, and found a bag of lemon drops hidden there, like in "Somewhere over the Rainbow". I smiled and popped one into my mouth before offering the bag to Grace. It really did feel like my troubles were melting away, like it said in the song – we'd dealt with the new spa opening, and the London orders would be piling in soon enough. Perhaps we'd be able to pay Mr. Vulmer *six* months' rent in advance rather than three – that would give us even more security.

We were really hungry by half five (even Dad, even after the ton of spag bol he'd eaten for lunch), so I got inventive with his half-empty fridge and made some cheese-and-mushroom omelettes with loads of toast.

After we'd eaten, Grace and Dad went back to designing the web page. I helped them as much as I could by writing out all the product information for the new range, as well as coming up with a few lines introducing the Rainbow Beauty brand. But at about half eight I collapsed in front of the telly, happy to see them working so closely together, both with the exact same looks of frowny concentration on their faces.

We were all surprised when the bell rang an hour later and it turned out to be Saff. Dad went to let her in, and followed her back to the sitting room, saying, "But, love, why didn't you text? I said I'd come and meet you."

"It's no big deal," she mumbled.

When she asked who'd like tea, Grace and I said "Hi" and "Yes please". But from the way she was banging around in the kitchenette, I started to wonder what was up. Grace didn't seem to notice anything, though, and soon she and Dad were side by side at the little table, engrossed in the website stuff sgain. Saff came in and put the tea down, glanced at them and went out again in silence. I thanked her for mine but she didn't even seem to hear. Then suddenly, completely out of nowhere, she stormed back into the main room and went into meltdown.

"Well, I didn't think *you'd* forget so quickly, Grace," she snarled. "Don't you feel like you're betraying Mum, cosying up with *him*?"

"Saff, what's going on?" Grace asked, looking uneasy.

But Saff didn't reply. Instead she turned on Dad.

"Oh, you think it's all fine now, don't you?" she snapped. "You've got us all back, like nothing happened. And now you're getting in on *our* new business too – how *perfect* for you!"

For a moment Dad just stared at her, and I thought he'd say something to calm her down. But then he just exploded. Grace and I stared at each other in alarm. It was so unlike him to fight back.

"No, I'm not having that!" he shouted. "Nothing's *fine*. Nothing's *right*. I miss you three every second of every day. I'm even missing you now you're here because I know that tomorrow you'll be gone and God knows when I'll see you again."

Saff looked really taken aback. "Dad, I—" she began.

But by then words were pouring out of him. "I regret *everything* that's happened, and I feel so, so guilty and I wish I could change things, but I can't, and that kills me. And if you want to know why I'm so engrossed in YOUR business, it's because I'm desperate to do everything I can to help make it work for you. And...and..." He faltered, and shook his head, like he'd decided not to say anything more.

But then Grace spoke. "Go on," she said gently.

Dad sighed. "And because I'm terrified that if I don't get up and showered and shaved and started on all this the second I wake up in the morning, I'll go back to where I was before I got this chance. Back down that black hole. Feeling pathetic and useless. Or worse, feeling nothing at all, some days. And that was a very dark and scary place, where I never want to be again."

My heart started pounding, hearing him say that. I thought back to how the bedsit was when I first saw it – filthy and dingy, with rubbish everywhere and the curtains closed in the middle of the day. Dad had been a mess too – unshaven, with dirty old clothes on and hardly able to make himself a cup of tea.

Saff had been there too, had seen the state of him, and now she looked horrified. "Dad, I'm so sorry. I didn't mean it," she gabbled. "I had no idea I even *felt* that way. I mean, I don't feel that way, not usually. All that just came out…"

Dad sighed. "I'm not telling you this to try and get sympathy," he told her. "You've every right to be angry – to feel *however* you feel. I'm just saying it because it's a fact." He rubbed his hands over his face and sighed. "Look, I'm going for a walk. Just for a few minutes. I need a bit of time alone, okay?" And with that he strode out without even picking up his jacket. I think he was about to cry, and he didn't want us to see.

After the door had shut behind him, Saff, Grace and I were just silent for a while. We were in shock, I think.

Finally, Grace said, "Look, Saff, it's not that everything's been forgiven and forgotten…"

Saff flopped down on the sofa and I put my arm round her. "I know," she said. "I wish I hadn't said all that now, but when I saw you all… Well, this anger just boiled up inside me. I really thought I was fine with Dad now. It just came out of nowhere."

"You probably just *wanted* to be fine so much that you really thought you were," I said.

Saff shrugged. "I guess I feel much more angry about everything than I realized," she said.

"Must have been hanging out with all those stage-school kids tonight," Grace joked, "bringing out your inner drama queen."

She was only trying to make Saff smile, but Saff said, "Maybe it was, in a way. Seeing my friends again made me realize just how much I miss my life here. And then coming in and seeing Dad there with you two, like everything was okay, when he'd taken all that from me, taken everything from all of us..."

"He couldn't help his business failing," I said softly.

"I know, but he *could* help lying about it, and having an affair, and leaving Mum, and forgetting to mention that the house was about to be repossessed." The anger rushed into her voice again.

"We're *all* still upset about what happened," said Grace. "It *is* a big deal, Saff, to all of us. No one's taking it lightly. We're just trying to find a way to move on, that's all."

"I know," Saff mumbled. "And I know Dad's trying really hard to make things up to us. Oh, I wish he hadn't gone off like that. I really want to talk it over with him."

We waited up for a while, but Dad didn't come back. It got cold and we couldn't find the heating control, so just after half ten we all climbed into the saggy old bed with the scratchy brown cover and snuggled together.

Saff and Grace fell asleep after a while but I couldn't because, for a start, they were taking up all the space and I was hanging off the edge, but mainly because I was worried about Dad. Just as I was about to wake my sisters and suggest calling the police or something, he crept back in.

"Dad!" I gasped with relief. "Thank God! You've been over an hour! I was starting to think all sorts..."

"Sorry, love," he whispered. "Once I started walking, I couldn't seem to stop. I just had to clear my head, that's all. I'm still struggling... But I know you girls are too. It's no excuse."

I slid out of the bed and tiptoed over to him. I gave him a big hug and he hugged me back. "Look, Saff didn't mean those things," I began.

"Yes, she did," he said flatly.

"Well, okay, she did, but she didn't mean *only* those things. Look, talk to her in the morning."

Dad gave me another hug. "What would I do without you, Abs?" he said.

"You don't have to worry about that, because you'll never *be* without me," I told him.

"Oh, love..." he began, but then there didn't

seem to be any more words, so we just smiled at each other in the orange glow from the street light outside.

Now I knew that he was safely home I just felt so exhausted I *had* to sleep. Saff and Grace had expanded into the entire bed space by then, so Dad insisted I have the sofa. He lay on the rug instead, using his jacket for a blanket, claiming that the floor was the best thing for his dodgy back anyway.

"Night, Dad. I love you," I told him, already half asleep.

"I love you too, Abs," he said. His voice went a bit wobbly, and in my mind I could see the tears sliding down his cheeks.

Well, as you can imagine, things were a bit awkward on Sunday morning. Dad seemed determined to be cheerful, though, and when Saff tried to say sorry again, he just brushed it off. "I really want us to enjoy the time we have together," he said. "I've been so looking forward to it. Let's just have a lovely morning, okay?"

"Okay," said Saff, looking relieved.

"So," said Dad, "your coach isn't till half two, is it? There's a whole big, beautiful city out there — what would you like to do?"

"Shopping!" cried Saff. Predictable.

And then of course we all got carried away, suggesting lunch out in the West End, a movie, a trip on the London Eye…

"Well, that's all out of budget," said Dad, "but I know where we can have just as much fun for free. Come on."

"Where are we going?" Saff demanded.

"Surprise," said Dad, winking at her. He pulled up his cuff to check his watch and his silver cufflink chinked against it. This was our old dad back again – smart, savvy and completely in control. "Grab your stuff, there's a bus in ten minutes."

Dad kept the surprise to himself all the way into town and we were really excited when he herded us off the bus at Covent Garden. As we linked arms in a big line and headed into the crowded piazza, Dad said, "*Et voilà* – all the shops, entertainment and delicious food you could want. Well, window-shopping, street theatre and Cornish pasties, anyway."

"Great idea," I told him, as Saff dragged me off to look in Oasis. We tried on half the shop and had a real laugh even though we couldn't afford anything, while Dad and Grace browsed in the bookshop just down the street. Then we met up and got steaming coffee and pasties, and ate them while watching this brilliant sword swallowing-juggling-comedy act by the church.

After that, we walked round the different levels of the piazza, looking in all the little shops and stalls, and of course we spent ages in Lush. I was in heaven surrounded by all the gorgeous products.

When we came out, we found Saff waiting outside for us, eyeing up a lad and giving him her most flirty smile. He was just coming over when Dad appeared in the shop doorway, immediately clocked what was going on and gave him such a death-stare that he pretty much *ran* in the other direction.

"Oh, thanks very much, Dad!" said Saff, pouting.

"No one looks at my princess like that," Dad grumbled, still glaring at the boy as he disappeared round the corner.

Well, Saff couldn't help smiling, and she only pretended to be put out for about two more seconds before taking Dad's arm and leading him off to look in the window of Ted Baker. I smiled too, glad that things were okay between them again.

As Grace and I followed behind, talking about which things we'd liked the most in Lush, I felt a huge wave of happiness inside me. I just loved the buzz of London so much and clearly my sisters did too.

But I didn't love it as much as Totnes, I realized. In fact, I was already starting to look forward to seeing Marco the next day at school, and Summer and Ben. And to me and my sisters all squashing up on our revolting brown sofa and getting an update from Mum on how things had gone at Rainbow Beauty while we'd been away.

I'd already started thinking about how to package the men's shower gel for Massimo too, and I was keen to get started on working out exactly the right combination of essential oils to make it really deep and rich. I couldn't help smiling to myself. Here was the whole of London spread out in front of me, and it was great – but it wasn't *home*, not any more. Home was our shabby little flat. Home was Rainbow Beauty, and Cavendish High, and Marco and my friends. Home was gorgeous, slightly crazy Totnes.

We were all a bit quiet on the coach, and I thought maybe Grace and Saff were still going over what Saff had said to Dad, like I was, and wondering when they'd see him again. We cheered up as we walked back to the flat, though, imagining Mum's face when we told her about the visit to Beau and what Massimo had said about our new range, and about him reordering the lime and ginger scrub, and actually *commissioning* me to come up with a men's shower gel. We burst in at about nine, brimming with chatter, only to find Mum sitting at the kitchen table, staring into space, looking ragged with exhaustion.

"I *knew* I should have stayed to help you," I cried.

"Don't be silly, love," she said. "I'm just tired, that's all. I'm glad you went. Now, tell me everything."

Grace started talking through our new orders and what Massimo had said, and Saff asked if there was any supper going.

"Oh, I haven't even thought about eating," Mum said. "Sorry, girls. I don't have anything in. I could probably rustle up a bit of cheese on toast..."

"You stay there," I told her. "Saff can get it."

"Oh, yeah. Saff can get it!" my sister grumbled, opening the fridge anyway. "Saff who's been busy all day, looking fabulous and being irresistible to boys! *I'm* the one who's exhausted."

Mum barely smiled at that, and then only nodded along as Grace told her about the shower gel costings. Although my sisters seemed to have taken it at face value that she was just tired, I started to get an uneasy feeling. For a start, she looked all pale and trembly, and like she was about to burst into tears at any minute.

"Mum, if something was up, you'd tell us, wouldn't you?" I said.

She sighed deeply and tears sprang into her eyes. "Oh, Abbie…I was hoping to keep it to myself until tomorrow at least, but…I saw this today."

She pushed the local free paper towards me. It was folded over at a full-page advert for the Haven Spa. "Half-price body treatments, *plus* free manicure," I read, and nearly choked with shock.

Saff gasped. "They've copied our promotion, pretty much!" she cried. "Right, this is war! Let's match their offer. No, let's better it! That will show them where they can stick their—"

"We can't afford to," Grace cut in.

"Anyway, they've done a price promise," I said, handing the paper across to her. "Just to make sure we can never compete with them on that score. Look."

Saff read, "*We pledge to match or better the prices of treatments and the promotional offers of any other beauty establishment within a three-mile radius.*" They're talking about *us*! This is a direct attack!" she cried. "We need to go down there, Mum. Have a word with them. They can't *do* this!"

Mum sighed. "I understand how you feel, love," she said, "but technically they haven't done anything wrong. They're just promoting their business."

Saff sighed sharply and was about to say something else when Mum added, "And we'll just look silly if we go and fling accusations about. Promise me you'll stay well away from there."

Saff didn't answer for ages, but Mum kept eyeballing her until she huffed, "Fine. I promise." But she didn't look at all pleased about it.

"The paper came out on Thursday, so that explains what happened," Mum said then.

"What? *What* happened?" Grace demanded.

Mum sighed. "Things went very quiet on the offer front on Thursday afternoon and it was the same on Friday. I didn't say anything to you girls, because I thought it was just a lull, and that lots of people would walk in without booking. But they didn't."

"But you said things had been fine!" I cried. "I asked you, both nights, and you said!"

"Why didn't you tell us?" Grace murmured.

"I would have, but I didn't think there was anything to worry about," Mum insisted. "I thought I'd have a busy Saturday, with Emily rushed off her feet doing the free manicures, and everything would be fine. But only one more lady rang up to book in on Friday. And I didn't get any more bookings on Saturday, so it was very quiet in the end. And two of the bookings didn't actually turn up, which was even worse. I got everything ready and then felt awful as the minutes ticked by and I realized they weren't coming. And then I've been here on my own all today, worrying and wondering about that blooming Haven Spa."

"Poor you. It must have been awful," I said.

Mum sighed. "It gets worse, I'm afraid… I went for a walk round town this afternoon, to clear my head, and I saw that they've put their offer posters right over our leaflets—"

"They can't do that!" Saff gasped. "Right, I don't care. I'm going round there—"

"No, you are not!" Mum cried. "I know how you feel, though. I was furious too. I mean, it wasn't just on the trees and lamp posts – they'd done it on the noticeboards where there was plenty of room for both. That was deliberate, nasty sabotage."

I thought of all our hard work – Marco trudging round town with the leaflets, Ben going up to Dartington specially and Summer happily taking a stack to put round the village near her house. It really did feel like the new spa was personally attacking us. Grace still hadn't said anything. She just looked pale and shocked.

"If they're going to be so aggressive, I'm just worried that…" Mum began. Then she waved her hands in the air, blinking fast. We waited for her to carry on, but she shook her head and let the tears roll down her cheeks. My heart lurched and I put my arm round her.

"You're worried that they won't stop until they've put us out of business," Grace said flatly.

Mum nodded, sniffling. "I've had to dip into our rent fund already, just to pay that supplier invoice that was due," she murmured. "I thought I'd easily be able to find the money from the week's takings, but there wasn't enough left after all. I've cut our housekeeping budget, and only ordered the minimum of the new supplies we need for Rainbow Beauty, but still…"

"Dirty tactics, that's what this is," Saff grumbled.

"They won't wreck everything we've worked for," I said firmly. "We won't let them. We've got the London orders coming, remember? And as for Rainbow Beauty itself, we just need to come up with a new idea to get people through the door. Not another offer that the Haven Spa will beat or match, but something different – something that plays to our strengths."

"You're right," said Mum, managing a small smile.

"Like what, though?" asked Grace. All three of them looked at me expectantly, waiting for the answer to come tumbling out of my mouth.

But it didn't. At that moment my creative brain seemed to have crawled under the duvet, put its headphones on and gone for a very long lie-down. I guessed we should do the same. "Let's sleep on it," I said. "We're bound to come up with something in the morning."

So we all slopped around getting ready for bed, our excited mood completely gone.

Chapter Seven

It was nice to see my friends on Monday, but not even Ben's jokes, Summer's hugs or Marco's arm round me as we walked between lessons could make me feel better. They were all really shocked about the Haven Spa's hardball tactics. They were gutted for me when I explained that people had stopped coming in for our offer (and in fact seemed to have stopped coming in, full stop) and they were almost as worried about our rent fund as I was.

Marco got really angry and macho and said we should sue, Ben offered to go up there and come back with some dodgy illness, but Summer understood that there wasn't a lot we could do because, like Mum said, on paper the new spa offered similar things to us and had the right to promote them in whichever way they liked, even though it felt like a personal attack.

Marco asked me if I wanted to go into town with him after school (he was meeting Luke at Pete's cafe, where the gig had been) but I said I couldn't. My sisters and I hadn't been able to come up with a plan to combat the new spa's aggressive tactics, but as we'd set off down the road together that morning, we'd thought of something to cheer Mum up, at least. So, as soon as the bell went, Grace and I hurried straight home to put our plan into action.

Mum was still in one of the treatment rooms with a client as we got things ready, and Saff joined us half an hour later, bursting in and saying she'd run all the way, *even in these shoes*, to be on time after the stupid bus was late. Grace and I had been tidying the parlour so that Mum wouldn't have to do anything, and Saff helped us finish that off. Mum came out a few minutes later, and cheerfully made up her client's bill and then saw her out, before collapsing into a heap on one of the purple velvet sofas. "Oh, I've had a terrible day," she wailed. "There were three cancellations…"

"Oh, Mum, I'm so sorry!" I cried.

As Grace, Saff and I listened to the details, I had a deepening feeling of doom. Even with all our Rainbow Beauty powers, the storm cloud hanging over Mum was so big and black, I didn't think we had a hope of lifting it.

"It was probably just a coincidence that they cancelled," Saff said blithely. I know she was just trying to cheer Mum up, but Grace and I both cringed.

"Of course it wasn't!" Mum snapped. "How can you not be worried? We lost over half our bookings today, and the rest of the week is looking very patchy."

"Of course I'm worried," Saff snapped back. "But getting all moody about it isn't going to help!"

"Moody?" Mum cried. "Saff, I'm not *sulking*. I'm devastated!"

Before Saff could open her mouth and say anything to make Mum even more stressed, Grace dragged her into the kitchenette. Meanwhile, I found a way to send Mum off up to the flat, claiming that I couldn't find the stock sheets anywhere and saying that she must have left them somewhere upstairs.

When she'd gone (well, stomped off, complaining about me losing things) we rushed around getting the surprise ready. A few minutes later she stormed back down again. "Well, they aren't up there," she snapped. "You'll have to go and borrow Liam's printer and run off some more. Honestly, Abbie, that poor man's helped us enough without you having to go and ask for something else. He must be sick of the sight of us…"

She trailed off and gradually took in what we'd done. There were candles everywhere, and soft music was playing. She'd marched right past Grace and Saff, who were standing either side of the door. Grace had a special smoothie on a tray for her and Saff was holding a fluffy dressing gown and slippers. "Surprise," we all mumbled, feeling like the whole thing was a bit pointless.

Mum gasped and put her hands to her mouth. Tears sprang into her eyes. "Oh!" she gasped, her voice going all wobbly.

"We wanted to do something special for you," I told her.

"To show how much we appreciate everything you do," added Grace, walking over and handing her the drink.

"It's pineapple and blueberry, your favourite," said Saff, in a sad little voice.

"Oh, come here!" Mum cried, pulling her into a hug. "I'm sorry I snapped at you, love."

Saff smiled and handed her the dressing gown and slippers. "Don't worry about it," she said generously (usually she'd milk it and be sulky for at least an hour). She gestured towards the treatment room we'd prepared, and put on the soothing professional beautician voice she used for clients. "If you'd like to go and get changed and then make yourself comfortable, Mrs. Green, your therapists will be with you in a moment."

Mum raised her eyebrows at Grace and I, and wandered off, sipping her drink as she went. After a moment, we all followed her in. In the treatment room, there were more candles, relaxing music, and a blend of rose and geranium oils in the burner.

"Oh, my favourite scent," she said, taking a deep breath.

"You're having the same oils for your massage too," said Saff. "Right, up on the table please, madam." Mum lay down with no arguing. "Then there's a luxury pedicure with our Olive Grain Foot Scrub and Soothing Minty Foot Lotion, which Abbie's doing, while Grace looks after your nails, and gives you a hand massage with our skin-saving Carrot and Calendula Hand Balm. I've taught her everything I know. She's getting very good."

"That sounds great, but what about your

homework, Grace?" said Mum, sitting up again. "It's always Maths on a Monday, isn't it?"

My sister smiled sweetly. "Luckily I'm very, very bright, so I'll just quickly do it in the loos before school tomorrow," she said. "Now, lay back and relax – that's an order."

A couple of hours later, Mum was swanning around in the dressing gown, smiling serenely. She looked like a completely different person.

"That was an amazing treat, girls. Thank you so much," she said, as we headed off (she was so relaxed that she didn't even care about walking out the front door to go up to the flat still *in* the dressing gown).

I was just locking up after us, and looking in at our gorgeous beauty parlour, and Mum was in the street in her dressing gown, beaming and waving to Mr. Trewis from the corner shop, when suddenly it came to me...

I knew how we were different and special.

And I knew what we could do to compete against the new spa.

"Mum, I've got a plan," I said suddenly. Grace and Saff turned back to listen. "We should put on a pamper day, with a really personal, community feel,"

130

I told them all. "Everyone will get to see their friends and meet new people, have treatments and try out our products, and we could do a massage demonstration so they can have a go at home, and we'll put on a buffet lunch too. The new spa may have the latest equipment, but they don't have what we have – *us*!"

"Wow, Abbie, that's a fab idea," said Saff, straight away.

"I agree," said Grace. Then she added, "We'll need to think about how much to charge for it, though, because they'd probably want to just pay a set price, wouldn't they, for everything, and——"

"It *is* a great idea, love," Mum cut in. "But do you think we could discuss it upstairs, because I'm starting to feel a bit silly standing in the street in this dressing gown!"

So we all hurried up to the flat and I grabbed a notebook from my chill-out room while Saff kicked her shoes off and put the kettle on. Mum got changed and Grace got out her beloved calculator and began sharpening her pencils to neat points. Then we all sat down and worked out the details of the pamper day. My heart was thudding with excitement. I love it when ideas just happen, like magic – it makes me feel charmed, and invincible.

"So, Abbie, say what you said downstairs and let's write each point out separately, so we can talk about it," said Mum.

"Okay, well, there would be a chance to try out the products," I said. "And what about teaching them how to make the smoothies and fresh face masks? And each person could have a mini-treatment, like a head massage, facial or manicure – maybe they could choose from a list of four or something. We could do them in the main reception as well as using the treatment rooms."

"Hang on!" Mum cried. "What was that last one? Manicure?" she asked. I nodded and she wrote it down.

"We'd put on lunch," I continued. "You could make your lovely canapés, like you did for the grand opening."

"That sounds great!" Saff enthused.

"It does," Mum agreed. "Oh, Abbie, thank goodness for you! For *all* of you girls! I was feeling so down today, and you've completely turned things around."

"I just hope it works," said Grace.

"It will," said Saff confidently. "People love being pampered with their friends."

I smiled. "Look, I know we've been badly hit by

this new spa, but we've worked so hard to get Rainbow Beauty up and running, nothing's going to stop us now."

"I hate to say this, but one pamper day isn't going to make everything better," Grace began. "We're behind on our rent targets now. Way behind…"

"I know," I told her. "But it's a start. And if it goes well, we could have one a month. And don't forget the orders from the London side – they'll be coming in soon."

"*Flooding* in, I bet," said Saff. "It went so well with Massimo, I'm sure it will be the same with the other shops. Dad's had three more appointments today – he'll be racking up orders as we speak. Maybe I should ring him to get an update…?"

"Do if you like," I said, "but I know he's got meetings booked in for tomorrow and Wednesday too. Maybe we should leave him to it for now. He's probably travelling back to his flat at the moment."

"Okay," said Saff.

"We won't let this beat us," I told Grace. "No way."

"Let's do the ticket sales just by word of mouth, and at the Autumn Fayre, though," she said. "No posters or anything. If they get wind of this at the new spa, they'll just do something to sabotage it. We need to be clever."

"Good thinking," I said, and Mum and Saff agreed.

We decided to hold the pamper day on the first of October, so that we didn't clash with the big arts festival in town the week before. Saff had wanted to do it right away the following week, but Mum was worried we wouldn't have enough time to sell all the tickets – and we all agreed it had to be sold out. We set the ticket price at £25, including lunch and a mini-treatment, and agreed to try and sell fifteen tickets.

Then Mum said, "Right, now that's sorted, how about some tea?"

And when we sat down to eat half an hour later, I didn't mind that all the posh bits were missing from our cannelloni and it was just tomato pasta again. We had the London shops (I'd just sent the shower-gel sample off to Massimo along with the ten lime and ginger body scrubs he'd ordered), and we were expecting big things from Dad's pitches. And now, with the pamper-day plan in place, we had something special to offer our local clients, too. We were sure we'd get the rent money together in time, and get our mozzarella and crème fraîche back!

* * *

Getting on with the pamper-day stuff gave me a good feeling for all of Tuesday, and it lasted most of Wednesday too. I was also busy counting down the hours until we heard back from Dad. His last appointment was at four o'clock that day and he'd promised to call us straight after. Like Grace had said, the pamper day was a step in the right direction, but it was the London orders that would keep us afloat, and make up the main chunk of our rent payment. Grace and I rushed back from school and Saff got in just after us. Then it was pretty much a case of all four of us hovering round the phone on the reception desk. When it finally rang, I snatched it up.

"Hi, love," said Dad.

"Dad! Thank goodness!" I cried, automatically hitting the button for speakerphone. "So, did they love the new range?"

"How are the figures looking?" Grace cut in, grabbing up a pen and some paper from the reception desk. "Have we hit our targets? I know we were aiming for 200 initial orders, but I'm hoping it'll be more like 300."

"I have to stop you there," said Dad in a weary voice. "I'm afraid I haven't got good news. I've been to all my pitches now, and at every single one they told me the same thing. It seems that committing to a year-round range is much more difficult for them than we'd realized – our Beauty and the Beach products went into their promotional space, and that'll be filled with Christmas stuff soon, which they've already chosen. To get permanent shelf space is much harder, apparently."

"But Massimo loved them!" I cried.

"I guess we shouldn't have relied on the opinion of one single retailer," said Dad. "We should have checked with a few more. Well, I've done that now, and the results haven't been good."

"So what are you saying?" asked Saff anxiously. "They've still taken some, haven't they? Even if it's not as much as we'd hoped?"

Dad sighed deeply. "The rainbow theme didn't really help," he said then. "They felt they'd need to take some of each product to line them up nicely as a rainbow, and then if some sold through quicker than others it would be left looking bitty."

I really thought I was going to throw up then. "I suggested the core range, and had the rainbow idea," I stuttered. "This is all my fault."

"Don't be silly," Mum cried, putting her arm round my shoulders. "We all agreed. Your dad and I have more business experience than you, so if anything, *we* should have thought of these issues."

"We should have done citrus," said Saff. Unhelpfully.

"We should have just concentrated on the gift sets instead of trying to sell individual products, so they were all complete rainbows," said Grace.

We stared at her. She was right.

I groaned. "Why is it that things you completely miss at the time seem obvious afterwards?"

"We all missed it," said Mum. "Everyone makes mistakes in business. It's learning from them that matters." She smiled at me. Well, she tried to, but it went all wobbly. She was right – about making mistakes, I mean. But would we have *time* to learn from them?

"Dad, you didn't answer the question," Saff said then. "How many orders?"

There was a long pause. "I'm afraid only two shops have actually ordered *anything*," he muttered. There was stunned silence from our side. "And you're right, Grace," he said. "They did only go for the gift packs. One shop would like five and the other, three."

"Eight?" I gasped. "Is that it?" My stomach dropped into my shoes. The future of Rainbow Beauty was riding on the London orders. This couldn't be happening.

"The gift pack product sizes are smaller, so there's much less profit when you factor in all the packaging," said Grace. "We're hardly going to make any money!"

"I'm sorry, love," said Dad, and I heard his voice break a little. It must have been tearing him up to have to give us such bad news. "I tried my best, I promise you."

"I know you did," I said quickly. "We all know you did."

"Yes, we do," said Saff.

"Yeah," Grace mumbled.

Mum didn't say anything. She just looked dazed.

"It was my fault. The product was wrong," I muttered.

"No, it wasn't," Dad said firmly. "What your mum said was right – we all agreed on our strategy."

"And don't forget, Massimo liked them as they were," Saff reminded me.

"We can tweak the range now we've got feedback," said Grace. "We'll just do gift packs of all seven products, and make the sizes a bit bigger."

"I don't think I'll get another chance to sell them in to those shops," said Dad, "and the big stores haven't even returned my messages."

"Well, then you'll have to—" Mum began.

"I *did* go in," he snapped, cutting her off, "but the beauty-department buyers refused to see me without an appointment. It's so frustrating! How am I supposed to arrange one if they don't return my calls?"

I felt really sick and worried then. For the business, but for Dad too. This had obviously knocked all the confidence out of him. What if he got himself back in the awful state he'd been in when Saff and I first saw him in the bedsit?

"Liberty holds an open call for new suppliers every year," I said, trying to find something positive to say.

"True," Dad said. Then he sighed loudly. "Next spring, I think it is. Look, don't worry about this. If you send up the revised rainbow gift pack and costings, I'll just cast the net wider." We could all tell how disheartened he was, though.

"Well, did Massimo like the shower gel?" I asked, in a tiny voice.

"Yes, love, he did," said Dad, "and he'd like ten more please, so that's something."

"Good," I mumbled. Usually it would have been fantastic. But coming after such bad news, it felt like a really tiny amount.

We all told Dad we loved him (well, except Mum,

of course) and then rang off, and I spent the rest of the evening desperately wishing I could somehow magic myself to London to give him a big hug, without a six-hour journey, or missing school, which I knew Mum would never allow.

When the bell above the door jangled on Thursday after school, we were all in Rainbow Beauty, smiling and looking smart in our pink uniforms, ready for our very important visitor.

It had been Mum's idea to invite Mr. Vulmer, the landlord, over. "With the London hiccup, and this new spa, there's no way we're going to have the three months' rent that he wants," she'd said, as we sat quietly over supper the night before, still upset about Dad's news. "So rather than bury our heads in the sand, we'd better start talking to him about paying in instalments."

So she'd called him, and we'd made sure everything was shipshape in the parlour as soon as we'd got home from school – we wanted to show him how professional we were. He came wheezing through the door, and even with autumn in the air, he was still wearing one of his garish palm-tree-patterned shirts. I forced myself not to wrinkle up my nose at his signature scent, which was a mixture of stale bacon fat, sweat and cigarettes.

"Mr. Vulmer!" cried Mum, greeting him like an old friend. "Can I get you a cup of tea? We've got digestives in too, because we know they're your favourite."

"No thanks, Mrs. Green," he rasped, hardly even bothering to look at her (and completely ignoring me and my sisters). "I'm a busy man. Why did you call me round at such short notice? If it's the rat problem again, I told you, there's a box of poison under the—"

"No, no, the rat issue has been dealt with by a pest-control company," Mum said hurriedly. "Everything's been done completely professionally, and all approved by Health and Safety. As you can see, we have a very nice business going here."

He'd been peering around at the beautiful sofas and reception desk and granite smoothie bar and the glass shelves full of products. "I can see that," he said. "We should talk about increasing the rent now you've got yourselves up and running."

Saff made a sudden, half-choked noise and Mum looked panicked. She seemed to be trying to say something, but no words would come out. She gave Grace a desperate look and my sister stepped in.

"Actually, we did ask you here to discuss the rent," Grace said, sounding calm and breezy (I'm sure only *I* noticed her hands trembling slightly with nerves). "Being a businessman yourself, I'm sure you can appreciate that, as a new business, we've had a lot of initial costs to meet. We're only just recouping those now. So, to help with our cash flow, we'd like to pay you monthly, in advance of course, rather than in three-monthly instalments."

Mr. Vulmer peered at her, probably dimly remembering that she was the one who'd talked him into letting us rent the shop and the flat at such a low rate in the first place. But Grace's magic didn't work a second time. "No," he said flatly. "That's not possible. I need to know you're not going to take off at a moment's notice and leave me with this lot to sort out."

Mum looked furious at that, and I had to put my hand on Saff's arm because I thought she was going to fly at him. I should have stuck my other hand over her mouth though, because, "Why would we do that?" she snapped. "We've built up a business here. Our life is here. We're desperate to keep it going and that's why we're asking you to give us a bit of leeway. You'll get your money each month, but if you won't let us pay like that, well, you might not be getting any at all because—"

"All Sapphire is saying," said Mum, glaring at her and cutting in, "is that we're as keen to make this work as you are. So if we could just agree to pay monthly – and we could do direct debit, so you had the guarantee…"

Mr. Vulmer sneered. "I do cash only," he wheezed. "And I'll be round for my three months' rent for both the shop and the flat on the eighth of October, as we agreed. If you haven't got it, you go. End of."

Mum looked like she was about to burst into tears, and I wasn't sure how much longer I could hold Saff back for.

As Mr. Vulmer turned and lumbered out, none of us said anything. We just watched him, barely breathing, hardly moving. Then, when he'd disappeared from view, we all collapsed onto each other.

"What a hideous man!" Saff cried.

"He's being so unfair!" said Mum. "Most people pay their rent every month, or even weekly."

"You'd think he *wanted* the business to fail!" I grumbled.

"I think he does," said Grace quietly.

"What?" gasped Saff, rounding on her. "Why would you say that?"

Grace sighed. "Think about it. He's getting a pretty small rent from us, but the shop fit will have added thousands to the value of this place. If he chucked us out, he might be able to sell it, or rent it to someone else at a higher rate, or even just rip out all the fittings and sell them – I know we got everything cheap thanks to Liam, but this lot would be worth a fortune if it was sold off."

Mum, Saff and I just stared at her. I felt physically sick. "That can't be true, surely?" I stuttered. We've got to talk to him again, make him understand…"

Mum sighed. "The only language that man understands is money," she said. "We've got to have that cash ready for the eighth and then we'll probably have to agree to a rent rise to keep him off our backs."

"But we won't *have* the money," said Saff, stating the obvious.

Mum sighed. "It doesn't look like we will, no."

"There's still the pamper day," I said quietly. "I've sold quite a few tickets."

Mum gave me a proud, sad look, as if her heart was breaking. "That's great, hon, but without any decent London orders it's not going to make much difference…"

"I know," I murmured. "I know."

No one said it would be okay, and no one said we'd work things out, and no one came up with a miracle solution. In fact, we barely spoke, and after forcing down a thrown-together supper of scrambled eggs on toast, we all stumbled about, staring at the TV, flicking through magazines without taking anything in, and drinking endless cups of tea we didn't really want.

I couldn't get to sleep for ages that night, and when I finally did, I had horrible dreams about Rainbow Beauty being closed down. Everything was ripped out, and it was all dingy and dusty, with a pile of unpaid bills on the floor. The door was bolted and when we tried to get up into the flat, the locks had been changed. Our stuff had been piled up on the pavement, and we had absolutely nowhere to go.

Chapter Eight

Saturday — the day of the Autumn Fayre — was lovely and clear with a chill in the air. Even though I still felt awful about, well, pretty much everything, I had to pull on my clothes, and a smile — Summer needed me, after all. I'd promised Mum and my sisters that I'd sell my heart out (and promote my bottom off!), given them all big hugs and gone to call for Liam, who'd offered to take me and my stuff to Summer's place in his van.

When we got there, Liam stayed to help her dad, John, and her brothers set up the stalls. The Autumn Fayre was being held on a big bit of grassy garden past the vegetable plots at the back of the house. As well as the usual random chickens, plus Biff and Chip the dogs wandering around, there were loads of cars in the drive and people unloading things and lugging stuff about.

I put the blenders down on my stall, along with the posters we'd made, and once I'd waved goodbye to Liam I wandered into the house to find my best friend. Summer's house is one of those walk-in-the-door-and-shout-hello! ones, and I always get a warm feeling as I step through into the officially fabbest, maddest, messiest, cosiest kitchen in the world. A huge rack of bunches of herbs hung up by the ceiling, and the giant dresser was cluttered with mismatched china, boxes of strange teas and bits of artwork that looked like they'd been made in primary school by Summer and her brothers, and put up ten years ago. The big red Aga was topped with trays of muffins, cupcakes and brownies, cooling ready for the Fayre.

"Hi, Abbie! Help yourself," said Annie, Summer's mum, as she wandered in and saw me eyeing up the stove top.

"Thanks," I said. I reached into my blue denim skirt pocket and found 50p to donate. I was also wearing a purple top, pinky-purple leggings, and the gorgeous purple scarf Sienna had given me. Saff had even done my nails indigo, so I'd match my blueberry-themed stall from head to toe.

Summer came crashing down the stairs then, burst in and pulled me into a big hug. "You look great!" she cried.

"You look amazing!" I shrieked. She was in charge of the face-painting, and had started with herself, shimmering with pinks and purples, and wearing full hippy fairy gear – stripy tights, glittery DMs, tutu, tattered tie-dyed top, wings and all.

"Give me a hand taking these to the cake stall, would you, girls?" Annie asked. "People will start arriving in half an hour and I haven't even got the bunting up yet!"

Annie grabbed a pile of gorgeous vintage plates and platters from the dresser and we arranged the delicious goodies on them. We only had two of those dome things you put over cakes, but Summer had had the idea of improvising by covering the rest with some upturned glass mixing bowls and they looked really good too. Annie found the white paper bags and tongs and put them into the big pockets of her patchwork skirt and we set off for the cake stall, weaving our way through the runaway runner beans and the bright clumps of rainbow chard that grew right by the back door.

We reached the lawny bit and found that the Fayre was already taking shape. John was getting the spit-roast going, some young mums were organizing a bric-a-brac and baby clothes stall while their little ones toddled around on the grass, a couple of older ladies were sticking numbered tickets onto prizes at the tombola, and over in the field to the right, Carrot the donkey was getting a good brush down by Jim, Summer's brother, before his starring role giving donkey rides. The goats and sheep had been brought into a pen by the fence for petting too, though the chickens had obviously decided that they were staying *free range,* thank you very much, and had strutted off to investigate Summer's face-painting table. It looked gorgeous with all her colours and brushes and glitter sprays set out on it. She'd even put up some pictures along the side of the table of the kind of faces children might like to choose – there were tigers, lions, pandas, pixies, aliens, wizards and witches, and fairies, of course. "I could do you as a blueberry," Summer said, appearing at my side.

"Thanks, but I think I look like enough of one already," I told her. "Can you give me a hand with my stall? The Fayre starts in fifteen minutes and everything's still in boxes."

Summer linked arms with me. "Sure," she said. "Oh, today is going to be fantastic!"

When we'd finished my stall, it looked really cool. The posters of Ben with the blueberry mask on (and pulling a silly face) were so funny, and much better than if *I'd* been on them. Summer hadn't been joking when she said that she thought Tom the greengrocer would donate loads of blueberries. He brought over about forty punnets of gorgeous fresh indigo berries, glowing like jewels in the autumn sunlight (and we thanked him loads, of course). We left them in the wooden crates and just propped those up with some old bits of brick, to show them off. Then we set up the blenders and paper cups for smoothies, and Jed brought over a cool box of Annie's home-made yogurt, which was going into them, and sorted out an extension lead for us.

When we were all ready, we had a few minutes free, so Summer took me over to see the yurt. She and Annie had transformed it into an enchanted storytelling tent, with scarves hanging everywhere, and a huge papier mâché dragon curled around the floor cushions. The little fairy lights that Summer had put up for our last sleepover made the whole thing glow magically.

"Wow, Summer, it's amazing!" I gasped.

"We've got an actual storyteller coming," she said. "When we said the event was for charity, he offered to perform for free."

"That's really kind," I said.

"Yeah, everyone's been so amazing, helping us out," said Summer, as we ducked back out of the yurt...

...and pretty much fell straight into Ben and Marco.

"Hey, Abs," Marco drawled. I blushed about a zillion degrees, of course, and wobbled a bit, because seeing him always made my knees go completely collapsy.

"Hi," I said, and luckily it didn't matter that I could hardly stand up because he pulled me into a hug.

When we broke apart, and I regained the use of my legs, Ben was still staring at Summer in what I swear was a "me likey" kind of way.

"What?" she demanded, doing the goggly eyes thing at him.

Ben came to and grinned. "Oh, nothing. You've just got something on your face," he said.

"Ha ha," she said, swatting at him. Ben grabbed Summer's wrists and started on about her violent streak, and she aimed her DMs at his shins while he leaped out of the way, smirking. They jumped about two metres apart as Annie came hurrying up to us, though.

"Hi, boys! Thanks for coming," she said. "Sorry to rush you, but people are already arriving. So, Abbie and Summer, if you could take your places, and Ben, you're on donkey duty. Marco—"

"Sure thing," he cut in. "Summer told me I'm handling the spit-roast." He grinned at me and then strode away, saying, "Fire, meat — what's not to love?"

"Erm, change of plan," Annie called after him. "Ethel's not well, so we need you on the cake stall with Iris and Brenda."

Well, Summer and I totally killed ourselves laughing at *that*. Luckily her face-painting table was right next to my stand and we were pretty much opposite the cake stall, so we could keep on killing ourselves laughing as Iris and Brenda fussed over Marco, tying up his flowery apron and showing him just the right way to set out the price labels.

We had a good few minutes of giggling and going, "Oooooh, young man!" (while Marco had a big session of secretly flicking V-signs at us when Iris and Brenda weren't looking), before people started making their way across the lawn and we had to concentrate on what we were supposed to be doing.

Well, things got busy really quickly, and I was whizzing up and selling so many fresh face masks that another volunteer – Sue, from the cafe where Headrush did their last gig – had to come and take over making the smoothies for me. It was really fun, chatting to people about Rainbow Beauty. I gave out loads of leaflets, too, and it felt like our opening day again, when we'd gone to the town fayre and set up a stall. Lots of people were interested in the pamper day, and I sold three tickets for it within half an hour. But then I kept suddenly feeling really sick, thinking about the London disaster and what the new spa might do next, and how on earth we were going to find the next three months' rent for vile Mr. Vulmer by his horrible deadline. It was like being on a roller coaster.

Still, I just had to put it all out of my mind and concentrate on making the most money I possibly could for the hospice, so I smiled and chatted and sold my heart out. Our bags of Blueberry Wishes were selling really quickly too, although no one seemed to have heard of it before, so I guess it *was* just Summer's family tradition, and not the whole of Devon's, after all!

Summer had a queue of children at her table and soon there were little pixies and lions and aliens pinging about everywhere, and even a Harry Potter lookalike, with a painted-on lightning-bolt scar and glasses. We all worked solidly for the first couple of hours, and more and more people kept arriving, and it wasn't till about midday, when the spit-roast was ready and everyone made a beeline for it, that we had a quiet patch.

Sue said she was fine to look after my stall for a while, and Summer put a *Back in ten minutes* sign on hers and we grabbed Marco and headed over to the field to see how Ben was getting on. On the way we did a few more rounds of "Oooooh, young man!" and insisted that we saw him checking out Brenda's bum, just to wind him up. We found Ben running around the petting-zoo pen – the goats and sheep seemed to have joined forces to terrorize him.

"Summer, do something about your psychotic animals, will you?" he shrieked. "That goat's just tried to bite a hole in my shirt!"

Summer just about managed to control her laughter enough to get out her phone and take a few pictures. "I'm not coming in there," she giggled. "I don't want poo on these boots!"

"Summer! This is serious!" Ben yelled, as she doubled up laughing again.

I managed to control my giggles for a moment

and gave Marco a pleading look. He gazed down at his Vans sadly. Then he sighed and marched towards the pen, saying, "You shouldn't have sent a boy to do a man's job. Watch and learn, ladies. Watch and learn."

But as soon as the goats and sheep spotted Marco, they headed in his direction instead. They weren't even running or anything, just going to have a look at him, but he totally freaked out, doing a really girly scream, scrambling back to the fence and just throwing himself over it. It was so funny I could barely breathe from laughing. Marco landed in a heap in the mud by our feet, and Summer snapped another picture. "That's SO going on Facebook," she told him. "Not such a cool rock star now!"

"What were you saying, mate, about boys and men?" called Ben, who'd slipped out of the gate while the animals weren't looking. Marco just gave him the evils, then stood up and brushed himself off, grumbling.

"I thought you were on donkey rides?" Summer said to Ben.

"I was," he told her, "but Carrot's having a hay break because he was going non-stop all morning. I thought I'd help out with these, but they're vicious!"

"Only to you!" I giggled. A mum and small girl

were now petting the goats and sheep through the fence further down, and the animals were standing calmly, looking super-cute.

Ben scowled at them. Then he said, "Who's up for checking out the stalls?"

"I'd better get back to my table," said Summer with a frown, "or there'll be an angry mob of five-year-olds on my case." She hurried off, and Marco headed into the house to de-muddify himself, so just Ben and I went back to the main bit of the Fayre and wandered round.

We had a go on the tombola and when Ben drew a ticket ending in zero, he leaped around celebrating like a little boy.

"I wouldn't get too excited. It's not the lottery," I teased, wrinkling my nose up at him.

"Abs, you don't understand, I have never *ever* won anything in my entire life!" he cried. "I don't care what it is. Even if it's just a box of chocolates or whatever, I've *won* it!"

I grinned as one of the nice old lady volunteers matched the ticket with the right prize and handed Ben something pink and knitted and a little bit scary.

He took it, thanked her, grabbed my arm and pulled me away from the stall. "Oh my God, it's hideous!" he hissed. "What's it even *for*?"

"That, my friend, is your classic ballerina loo-roll cosy," I told him, smirking. "Last seen in a bathroom circa 1985."

Ben squinted at it. The spooky-looking half Barbie doll on top seemed to be staring back at him in an evil way. "I think this one's haunted," he said. "And who wants to keep a loo roll *warm*, anyway? Isn't that a bit pervy?"

I shrugged. "You could always wear it as a hat."

Ben put it on and pulled a pouty fashion-model face.

"That actually really suits you," I giggled, and we ambled over to the coconut shy, where he took the loo-roll cosy off his head so he could concentrate properly on winning one of the non-scary cuddly toys on offer.

Ben had hit two coconuts out of two, and was about to go for his third throw and win himself something less awful than the loo-roll cosy, when I decided it was the perfect moment to strike with my suspicions about him and Summer. My theory was that as he was concentrating so hard on something else, he'd just give me a straight answer without even thinking about it.

Clever, huh?

Well, not so much, as it turned out. Just as he was

about to throw, I said, "So, things are hotting up between you and Summer."

What actually happened is that he whirled round to face me mid-throw and if I hadn't had such quick ducking reactions from years of living with Saff, her temper and her flying shoes/biscuits/teddies, he'd have taken my head off. "What do you mean?" he demanded.

"Woah, steady on!" I cried. "I just meant that I'm glad things are okay now. You know, after what happened at the beach party—"

Ben glanced sharply behind us, to where Jim and Jed, Summer's big brothers, were lazing on the grass, stuffing down baguettes full of spit-roast pork. "Oh my God, keep your voice down!" he hissed. "They don't know, do they? About what happened?"

"No, course not," I whispered. Then I added, "If they did, you'd be dead by now." I was joking, obviously, but Ben just looked terrified.

I sighed. "Look, I've noticed, lately, you and her... Well, I wondered if something..."

"Nah, you've got that wrong," he insisted. "I'm not into Summer. And even if I was, just in theory, she wouldn't be into me anyway, not after what happened at the beach party." He cast another nervous glance at Jim and Jed.

"Well, I wouldn't be so sure about that," I said. Uh-oh. That mouth of mine again. Going too far, as usual. But I was glad I'd said it, because Ben stared at me and demanded, "What? Has she said something to you? What's she said?"

Well, that was way too intense for someone who wasn't bothered. "No, nothing...she hasn't said anything," I insisted. "Not *as such*."

Ben huffed about a bit then, saying, "Well, you're probably just imagining things. I know what girls are like, seeing stuff that isn't there. Not that it matters what she thinks anyway because I'm not into her in that way."

I rolled my eyes. "I know. You said. *Several times*. Look, there's no queue now. Why don't you have a go at the coconuts again?"

"Too right," said Ben. "I'm not leaving this stall until I win something proper."

It didn't take long, actually. He hit three coconuts just like that – bam, bam, bam – in quite an impressive manly way. And then he chose the most *unmanly* prize on offer – a little purple sparkly unicorn.

"Good choice," I teased.

"It's for Gabe, not me!" he said, giving me a despairing look. "Come on, we'd better get back to work."

* * *

The Fayre finished at two, and John and Annie gathered us all together to thank everyone, and we gave them a huge clap too, for organizing such a great event. They said they didn't know exactly how much we'd raised, but it looked like being close to £2000 – well, everyone went mad about that, clapping and cheering and the blokes doing that back-slapping "good one mate" thing. Except Marco, that is, who got hugged by both the cake-stall ladies at once! I was pleased that all our leaflets had been taken, too, and from chatting to people, I was pretty sure I had seven definites and at least five maybes to book in for treatments. I'd also sold a grand total of eight pamper day tickets.

I was staying on at Summer's to help clear everything up, and then sleeping over, because we'd planned to work on our presentation for English on Sunday morning. I thought Marco and Ben might stick around for a while too, but Ben had to head off to his conservation group at Dartington Hall and Marco was meeting his dad at Rocket.

"You don't mind, do you?" Marco asked, pulling me close.

"No, course not," I insisted. "It's great you're spending time together." He pulled me into a hug and gave me a quick, non-snog-type kiss.

I hugged Ben goodbye and then Marco grabbed Summer and did that kind of headlock-while-swinging-from-foot-to-foot thing they always do, because they're too much like brother and sister to have a normal hug. Then Summer went to say goodbye to Ben, and he obviously thought they were hugging but she went for cheek-kissing, and it ended up in a strange squashed embrace.

"Alright, don't suffocate me!" he grumbled.

"Well, I thought you were doing the cheek-kissing thing," huffed Summer.

"Since when have I done the cheek-kissing thing?" Ben demanded. "I *never* do the cheek-kissing thing!"

Summer sighed crossly. "Well, you sort of lunged at my face, so I thought—"

"I didn't *lunge*!" Ben protested. "It's this potholey path, making me tilt!"

"You're blaming my path for your lungey-ness?" she shrieked. "Go on, bog off, the pair of you! See you Monday, yeah?"

"Whatevs," said Ben.

"Yeah, see you!" called Marco. He didn't seem to have noticed anything unusual between Ben and Summer. But then, boys don't really notice *anything*, do they? Not unless you make a massive banner and hang it in front of them.

As the boys headed off across the lawn, Summer must have been watching me watching Marco, because she said, "Is it worrying you? Him and his dad?"

"I don't know," I told her. "It was, at first, but maybe Luke is really staying this time."

Summer followed my gaze. "Well, it still worries me," she said. Then she linked arms with me and we headed over to clear up her table.

"Oh!" she gasped, picking up the little purple unicorn she'd found sitting amongst the face paints. She cuddled him close. "He's gorgeous!" she cried.

"Ben won him," I told her. *For Gabe? Yeah, right!*

"I had my eye on this little one when we were setting up," she told me. "I said to Ben that I can't chuck a ball to save my life..."

"So he won him for you," I said.

Summer smiled at the little unicorn. "Yeah, I guess so. He's such a good mate."

I wanted to say that maybe he could be more than a mate, but just then Annie called us over to help carry in the tables, and after that there were always people around and things going on, so we didn't get a chance to talk properly until the sleepover.

* * *

At about seven o'clock, we had one of those shared suppers that seem to emerge from nowhere at Summer's, the table just suddenly filling up with rice and bean salads, bread, cheese, cold meats and a quiche made with eggs from the random wandering chickens.

As we all sat round, I ended up talking about the pamper day, and suddenly Annie was offering to do the lunch.

"Oh, wow. Are you sure? That would be amazing!" I said.

"Yes, of course," she said. "Your mum will have far too much to do on the day without thinking about the food as well. And I'll do some cupcakes and brownies, too."

"Put me down for a ticket," Jill, Annie's friend, cut in. "It sounds like great fun. I'll tell everyone at Am Dram Club tomorrow as well, and I expect you'll get a few more takers from that."

I couldn't help beaming then. The pamper-day tickets were selling like hot cakes. I knew it wasn't magically going to save Rainbow Beauty, but it gave me a real lift. Jill bought her ticket on the spot, and then we all had a small friendly row about whether Annie was paying for hers – I insisted she wasn't and she insisted she was, as we were still a new business.

I gave in in the end, because she pretty much forced the money into my hand, and also, I didn't fancy being on the receiving end of Grace if she heard I'd given a ticket away for free.

Then, once our faces were completely and utterly stuffed, and I'd thanked Annie again about ten times for offering to do the food, Summer and I headed out to the yurt.

We were carrying candle lanterns, our sleeping bags and a couple of big hoodies scrounged from Jed. Jim had lit the wood burner for us and we found that Annie had sneaked in and left us a basket with a flask of hot chocolate in it, and a couple of punnets of blueberries left over from the Fayre, as well as the last brownies from the cake stall and some incense sticks. Summer was still in her fairy regalia, and when we unravelled our sleeping bags to get inside so we'd be extra cosy, I found that she'd tucked the little unicorn into hers, and now she sat him on her lap and fiddled with his purple mane.

I'd been so desperate to talk to her about Ben all day, and seeing the unicorn make another appearance and everything, well, I just found myself wading in. "It was lovely of Ben to win that for you," I said. "Anyone would think he had a crush on you, and what with the way you two flirt all the time..."

Summer gave me a scandalized look. "We don't!" she cried. "He winds me up and I try to injure him. That's not flirting!"

But I wasn't giving up that easily. "And things used to be so easy between you, but now there are these awkward moments, like when you said goodbye today. It's *so* like me and Marco were before we got together…"

"Abs, you're imagining things!" Summer insisted. "Yeah, I did like Ben, you know I did. But that was just a silly summer-crush thing. Like I said, I'm completely over it now. And anyway, in case you've forgotten the hideous disaster at the beach party, *he* doesn't like *me* in that way. Look, I'm just glad it's over with, so there's no need to bring it up again, yeah?"

"Yeah, sure, whatever," I said.

Then she gave me a quick glance and mumbled, "I mean, unless he's actually *said* something…"

Huh! That was almost the same as what Ben had said, when he'd thought *she* might have said something. But I was careful not to let my mouth run away with me again. I'd made a mistake before, telling Summer that Ben liked her, just because *I* was sure of it. This time I was double-triple surer than sure, but I didn't dare risk saying anything – not until he'd actually admitted it to me. And maybe even signed some kind of form or something.

And as for Summer, I was 110% certain she was still into him, but 120% certain she'd never admit it without absolute proof that he liked her – not after her humiliation at the beach party. So, reluctantly, I made myself leave it alone for the time being.

We chatted for a while about school and stuff, and I got her to try the new Jasmine and Bergamot Hand Lotion I was working on (which she loved, BTW, so that was good!). Then I ended up talking about Rainbow Beauty, and how much we were struggling in the parlour, and how badly Mum was taking losing customers to the Haven Spa – how badly we were *all* taking it. And of course she knew about the disappointment we'd had with the London orders too, and Mr. Vulmer refusing to budge on the rent, and she said again that she wished she could do more to help.

"You *are* helping, just by supporting us," I told her.

"And I'll be on hand at the pamper day, of course," she said, "even if I just take people's coats and stuff."

I gave her a smile. "Thanks," I told her. "Maybe you can make the smoothies or something?"

It was really private and cosy round the wood burner, and I felt so at ease with Summer. Honestly, I'd just been feeling so happy, thinking about how much I'd done to promote Rainbow Beauty at the Fayre, and how many pamper-day tickets I'd sold, and then suddenly I found tears running down my cheeks. "Oh, Summer!" I gasped. "I'm just so scared about how badly things are going, and there's nothing I can do about it!"

She shuffled her sleeping bag over and pulled me into a hug. "You'll find a way through," she said. "You always come up with something."

I sighed. I felt like I'd used up all my ideas – all my nine lives.

"Make a Blueberry Wish," she said suddenly.

I shook my head, feeling hopeless. "Wishing won't help."

"Well, it won't do any harm," Summer insisted. She reached into the basket, counted out ten blueberries and tipped them into my hand. "Out loud, don't forget," she reminded me.

I gave her a small smile. "Fine. Just for you," I said. I ate the blueberries one by one and then said, "I wish for Rainbow Beauty to survive. I don't see how it will, though, so...I guess I wish for some kind of miracle. Right, you next."

Summer picked out ten blueberries and ate them, then said, "I wish that..." She paused and shook her head, as if she was trying to shake a thought out of it. Then she said, "I wish Jim would stop snoring at night. I can hear him through the wall, and they're about two foot thick in our house!"

I peered at her. "That's not what you were about to say..." I accused. I was certain she was going to wish that Ben liked her, or that they'd get together.

"It was!" she cried. "It's no joke. Jim sounds like an elephant with sinusitis. I can't get any decent sleep!"

"Hmm," I said, giving her a stern look.

Then I realized I needed a wee, and I tried to just go outside on the grass like Summer did, but for a start it was cold, and plus I was worried that someone might decide to look out of the window right at that moment. Then, just when I'd scanned the house about three times and bobbed down, I glanced towards the field. "I can't go – there's a goat staring at me!" I shrieked.

Summer popped her head out of the yurt and I bolted upright, whipping my leggings back up. "Goats don't have Facebook, you know!" she teased.

"I don't care. It's got eyes!" I screeched.

"Come on then, city girl!" she giggled. She linked arms with me and together we stumbled back towards the house. I snuggled in close to her and we matched our steps, like Grace and I always do.

Chapter Nine

I was glad to get off to school on Monday, as I'd arrived back at the flat on Sunday afternoon to find a cloud of gloom hanging over everyone. Saff had told me that on Saturday, four people hadn't turned up for their appointments and, as we weren't even fully booked in the first place, Rainbow Beauty had felt like a ghost town. The good news about the Autumn Fayre going well, and selling loads of pamper-day tickets cheered them up a bit, though.

Unfortunately, Monday wasn't any better at Rainbow Beauty, and when Grace and I got back on Tuesday after school, Saff told us that Mum had been really upset all day as they'd rattled around the near-empty parlour together, even though she'd tried to put a brave face on things. Just as Saff was saying that, Mum walked in and we quickly changed the subject, acting like nothing was wrong. Mum said she wasn't feeling well and went to bed early.

On Wednesday, she woke up with an awful cold. She still got up and dressed as usual, but looking at her slumped at the kitchen table, sweating and shivering, we could see there was no way she could work. After a bit of an argument, Saff managed to get her to go back to bed, and Grace and I went downstairs to call her clients. Of course, with no one to cover for her, we had to cancel their treatments.

Saff said she'd miss college and handle the manicures and pedicures so we didn't have to cancel those too (and told us not to mention that to Mum or she'd go mad), but even that didn't help. The two people who were booked in for manicures were having body treatments as well, and the first one Grace spoke to said she'd rather just cancel the whole thing. I realized why when I spoke to the other lady, who said she'd cancel too. "Don't worry, love, I'll go to the Haven Spa instead," she said cheerily. "They're offering a free manicure with a half-price massage." (Like, as if we didn't *know*!)

Hearing that made my stomach start churning and I felt like being sick, but I had to pretend not to mind, and say, "Oh, that's a very good deal. I hope you enjoy it." What on earth would Mum say when she found out no one was rebooking with us, and that we were basically handing our existing clients over to the new spa?

Even worse, a couple of people didn't pick up the phone, so we just had to leave messages and hope they got them in time. The very absolute worst call was the one I made to a lady who'd really wanted a massage and facial that day, because she'd got the day off. She asked me whether I could recommend anywhere else she could go at short notice and I found myself actually *suggesting* the Haven Spa and *telling* her they had an offer for a discounted body treatment and free manicure.

Grace glared at me when I hung up. "Oh, great! Now you're doing their advertising for them!" she hissed.

"What else could I say?" I snapped. "It wouldn't do Rainbow Beauty any good for me to be unhelpful and just say, 'Erm, don't know'. If you're going to criticize, you do the rest then!"

"Fine, I will…or we'll never get anyone back," she muttered as she dialled.

"Well, cheer up first or they won't be returning for our warm, friendly service!" I countered.

"Shh!" she hissed.

We glared at each other for a moment, until the client picked up at the other end of the line.

In fact, Grace didn't have any more luck than me with the next call. Trish, a regular client – the one who Mum had been on a girls' night out with – was the only person who said it was no problem and that she'd rebook when Mum was better.

After the hideous phoning ordeal, Grace and I dragged our way back up the stairs to the flat to get our stuff for school. She looked as sick as I felt. "What on earth are we going to tell Mum?" I hissed as we reached the top step.

"We're not," said Grace firmly. "She's feeling bad enough as it is. She'll be asleep by now. Let's just creep in and get our stuff—"

But Mum was leaning on the door frame of our shared bedroom, back in her dressing gown, and looking dreadful. "How did it go with the clients?" she asked.

Grace gave me a quick glance and we both put on big fake smiles.

"Oh, good, yes, all sorted," I told Mum. "Trish asked us to say she hopes you get well soon. She'll rebook when you're better, no problem."

"Oh, that's nice," said Mum.

Grace and I tried to make a dash past her into the kitchen for our schoolbags, but she said, "And the others? Were they okay to rebook too?"

"Yeah, absolutely. It's all fine," said Grace. Not very convincingly.

Mum sighed. "It's awful, isn't it? Abbie, tell me the truth."

She looked right into my eyes, and I knew there was no way I could lie. My stomach sank into my shoes. "Yes, it's awful," I told her. Then Grace and I summarized the awfulness. All of it. The cancellations, the rush to the new spa, the fact that I'd actually had to point someone in their direction.

Mum looked shocked for a moment, then went all determined. "Right, ring them back. I'm working today," she said, striding into the kitchen. But then she stopped by the table, swayed and clutched the back of one of the rickety chairs. I raced over and held her up.

"Mum?" Saff cried, emerging from the bathroom. "You're meant to be in bed."

"I'm going to work," she insisted.

"No, you're not. You're about to faint! Sit down," Grace ordered.

"I'll be fine," Mum muttered. She was dripping with sweat, and shuddering with chills. It was starting to look like more than just a cold. Maybe she had the flu, or a nasty virus. Whatever it was, she wasn't going anywhere.

As Grace put the kettle on to make Mum a hot drink, Saff took one arm and I took the other and together we frogmarched her back to bed.

"Oh, we've got to face facts…this is hopeless," Mum said sadly, wriggling right under the covers as Grace brought her a cup of tea. "I'm sorry, girls. We were only just getting started before the Haven Spa opened, and now I think we're doomed to fail. We'll have to close down Rainbow Beauty. I'll start looking for a job."

Tears sprang into my eyes and I felt panic rising in my chest. To hear Mum say that was awful…

Grace looked really wobbly too, but Saff just bundled us out of the room, saying we'd be late if we didn't get a move on.

My heart was still thumping as we all hurried down the road, and my legs were shaking so much I was glad I was in the middle, arms linked with Saff on one side and Grace on the other. "She didn't really mean that, surely?" I croaked, as we turned onto the main road.

"No, of course not. She's virtually delirious," said Saff firmly.

Grace sighed. "The problem is, success or failure is a spiral and we're spiralling the wrong way. If the Haven Spa hadn't opened, then maybe... But you saw today what a draw it is for our customers. Mum's right. How *can* we keep going with that on our doorstep? Mr. Vulmer can't wait to shut us down so he can get his hands on all the fittings and stuff, and we won't have the money to pay him on the eighth. We're nowhere near."

Well, that wasn't what I wanted to hear, not from sensible Grace, who knew all the figures for the business inside out. "We'll find the money somehow, though, won't we?" I asked again, this time hoping that her answer would magically be a *yes*.

Saff squeezed my arm and gave Grace a sharp look. "Abs, honestly, we'll find the money," she insisted. "And Mum will hopefully be better by tomorrow, and ready to take on the world again. Then there's only Friday until we're all there to help, and then just Monday till I'm there on Tuesday, and I'll be qualified in only—"

"Three years!" Grace snapped moodily.

"Yes, but I'll be able to do more and more treatments long before then, when I start passing the different modules," Saff snapped back, "and next year I get *two* release days a week. Look, instead of moping and talking about giving up, we need to put up a fight. We have to come up with some more unique offerings, let people know why we're different from the Haven Spa, and worth paying a bit extra for. I bet all *their* products aren't natural and home-made."

Grace sighed. "But we've tried offers – we just can't compete."

"I know," Saff admitted. "We need to come up with *something*, though. There's always a way, if you put your mind to it."

They both turned and looked at me expectantly, but I was completely out of ideas. And positive vibes. It felt hopeless. After all our hard work, all the love and care and passion we'd put into it, could we really be about to lose Rainbow Beauty?

At school I was too miserable to even have much of a flirt with Marco in lessons, and that's saying something. *Or* to scheme about how to get Ben and Summer together, even though I was now completely convinced that they were into each other. (Summer still insisted she wasn't, but she'd attached the little purple unicorn Ben won for her to her school bag. Say no more.)

When I told Summer about Mum being ill, and how I'd actually had to *recommend* the Haven Spa to one of our cancelled clients, she said she'd never seen me so miserable. "But what about all those people you spoke to at the Fayre?" she asked. "Didn't they make appointments in the end?"

"Five have booked for next week, but only three for this week so far, and I've just had to cancel one of those," I told her. "Eight new customers is good, of course, and I'd have been over the moon with that number if we weren't in such a bad situation, but the way things are, everything we do just seems too small to make a real difference. We need to find £2000 by the eighth, and at the moment we've only been able to put aside £550. No, actually, £462. Mum had to pay our business rates out of it." I sighed. "Maybe she's right and it *is* hopeless. I mean, we're probably going to be forced to close down by Mr. Vulmer in less than three weeks, so what's the point in even trying to drum up trade? We probably shouldn't even bother with the pamper day, but we've sold most of the tickets now, and we can't let people down."

I paused for breath and noticed that Summer was staring at me, looking shocked. "Abbie, you can't give up," she said. "You're the one who always says—"

"I'm *not* giving up," I assured her. "It's just that I'm all out of ideas, and time's running out."

She gave me such a look of sympathy and kindness I almost couldn't stand it. Luckily the bell went then, and I linked arms with her and hurried her into class so that we couldn't talk about it any more.

Thursday at school wasn't much better, especially when Jess asked me if she could buy some more Mandarin Body Butter. I had to tell her she couldn't – we'd run out, and there wasn't any money to order more shea butter for a new batch. In fact, there wasn't any money, full stop. Our takings from that week so far had gone straight out on an electricity bill that was on its absolute, final, pay-now-or-we'll-cut-you-off demand. Saying it to Jess made me feel sick. It was like the spiral Grace talked about – if we couldn't afford more ingredients, and couldn't sell more products, how on earth could we hope to make more money?

On Friday, I had to turn down three more requests for Rainbow Beauty products from Year 8 girls, because I knew we didn't have any in stock, and I was banned by Grace from buying ingredients to make any more. We'd somehow managed to save up an extra £100 for Mr. Vulmer by putting every scrap of what we'd made from clients' appointments on Thursday straight into our rent fund, and we were all absolutely banned from touching it.

Ben bought me an iced bun at first break (I hadn't wanted to ask Mum for any spending money), which I had to force down because I almost felt too sick to eat. At lunchtime Marco skipped a band meeting to hang out with me and try and cheer me up. It didn't work, but leaning against him on the field in a sort of sitting hug was nice – we had to move apart when Mr. Carver strode past and had a go at us, though. He started on about Inappropriate Public Displays of Affection (i.e. Being a Normal Teenager, IMHO. As Marco said, it's not *our* fault he's never had a girlfriend!). Summer said if it did come down to Mum having to find another job, she could put her in touch with loads of people her family know in town, like Pete and Sue at the cafe for a start. That was nice of her, but it actually made me feel worse, because then it seemed even more real.

I met Grace at the gate after school and we hurried back to Rainbow Beauty to help Mum out. She still wasn't well, not by a long way, but she'd insisted on working all day, and now she was sitting on one of the purple velvet sofas, looking completely spaced out. She'd only had three clients, and not a single person had come in for a smoothie or to buy any products, despite the chalkboard I'd put outside. As I threw away a pile of fruit that was way past its best, I went all trembly. But Grace and I just kept our heads down and got on with the tidying up, and soon Saff arrived and gave us a hand.

That was when Mum dragged us all over to sit with her on the sofas. The look on her face made me instantly nervous, though I couldn't possibly have foreseen the bombshell she was about to drop.

"Are you okay?" I asked.

"Something's come up," she said. "It's just an idea, and I hope you'll hear me out before you jump down my throat about it." She took a deep breath. "My friend Janine rang today. She knows what's happened, of course. Her, Peter and the kids are going to Canada for a year with his work. She wondered if we'd like to house-sit for them..."

Oh. My. God. I just stared at her – it was like she was speaking Japanese. Grace's face was frozen into a mask of horror. Even Saff was speechless. Janine's house was in Islington, as in Islington, *London*.

"*What?*" I gasped, after what felt like for ever.

"No way! We can't leave here," said Saff.

"We might not have any choice," said Mum flatly.

"We're not even close to having all the rent money for Mr. Vulmer, so we'll probably lose the flat anyway."

"We could get benefits," said Grace.

"I don't think so, not if we've still got the beauty parlour," said Mum. "And if we *haven't* still got the beauty parlour…" She paused, obviously finding it hard to go on. "Well, then, we might as well be in a rent-free house, building up the London side of things. Their kitchen is huge, more than big enough to make products in. And instead of sitting in a mostly empty beauty parlour, feeling more and more downhearted, I could be out selling our products with Dad – well, not *with* him, obviously, we'd kill each other, but *as well* as him."

She was trying to be funny, but none of us even smiled. Saff and Grace were looking anxiously at me and I was glaring at Mum. How could I leave my life…my friends…Marco? How could Rainbow Beauty not exist? I felt like storming off, but I knew I had to stay put and talk her out of this crazy idea.

"You cannot be serious…" I muttered.

"But why move back to London?" asked Grace, looking dazed. "We can make and sell products to retailers from here, even if we close down the treatment side of things for a while to focus on it."

"Grace, we don't have the money for the rent,

and Mr. Vulmer won't budge!" Mum cried, getting frustrated. "You know that as well as I do. I'm sorry to sound harsh, girls, but there won't *be* any 'here' in precisely sixteen days' time. We are going to be evicted, like it or not."

"You're giving up!" I accused. "You said we'd never do that and you *are!*"

Mum sighed. "No, Abbie. I'm actually trying to save the business, believe it or not. If we can keep making and selling products, there's a chance we can stay afloat and, who knows, maybe open another parlour in a couple of years' time."

I refused to nod or anything, but I knew what she meant. It was like when Jess had asked me for that body butter, and I'd had to tell her — and all those other girls — that we were out of stock. We were already running pretty low on other products at Rainbow Beauty — what would happen when we ran out altogether, or couldn't afford to order in more leg wax and nail files and body-wrap film? Things would grind to a halt.

"This opportunity has come up to have somewhere to live, rent-free, and keep the business going," Mum was saying. "I'd be mad not to consider it."

"Well, I suppose we'd be nearer to Dad," Grace said quietly.

I glared at her. Whose side was she on, anyway?

"Yes, there is that," Mum said. "Your dad would be over the moon."

I felt bad then, like I was being anti-Dad or something by wanting to stay. But what about Ben and Summer? What about *Marco*? Just thinking of losing them made me feel sick…. "But I don't want to—" I managed to croak, as tears spilled down my cheeks.

Mum winced when she saw I was crying and tried to put her arm round me, but I wriggled away.

"Well, you lot do what you like, but *I'm* not going back," Saff announced. "I like my course, and my tutor thinks I'm doing really well. I'll get some student accommodation. Maybe they'll let you stay with me too, Abs."

Mum looked horrified at that. "Oh, Saff, love," she said, "please, please don't say things like that." I could feel that she was desperately trying to catch my eye, but I still wouldn't look at her. "I know it's a lot to take in," she gabbled, "but just so you've got all the facts, you should know that I've checked and you could transfer to a London college with no problem, and you could enrol for a singing course at Arts Ed, just evenings – it's not nearly as expensive as the full-time one."

"I'm not interested," Saff grumbled, but she didn't sound outraged any more.

"How can you even *think* of leaving everything we've worked so hard for?" I asked Mum, still refusing to look at her.

"Abbie, we don't have a choice," she said flatly. "We have to face facts – Rainbow Beauty is beaten. Now we've got to save what we can and move on. And if we want to make sure we've got a roof over our heads, I'll have to let Janine know as quickly as possible."

I finally looked at her. "When?" I said quietly.

She looked awkward. "We can move in next Sunday."

"Next Sunday?" I shrieked. "But we can't!"

"And if we don't, the following Saturday Mr. Vulmer will come to collect a payment we can't possibly find, and then he'll throw us out," Mum said. "At least if we go the week before, it will give Liam the chance to sell off all the Rainbow Beauty fixtures and fittings, so that revolting man won't get his hands on them."

"But what about the pamper day?" I croaked.

"We can still do it as planned, on the Saturday," she said. "Lots of our regulars and friends are coming, so it will be a nice chance to say goodbye."

She smiled at me, as if that was meant to make me feel better. Instead, a swirl of fury rose up in my chest. My pamper-day plan was supposed to help save the business, and she wasn't even going to give it a chance. Instead she was turning it into our final farewell.

I glanced at Saff and Grace for support. "Come on, say something! Surely you two don't want to leave?"

"Course we don't *want* to," said Grace quietly. "But Mum's right. We can't afford to stay, or stay open. And this offer of somewhere to live won't come along again. I don't think we've got any choice."

I looked at Saff.

"Well, I suppose, if I can carry on my course up there…" she began, then trailed off and looked at the floor.

I couldn't believe it.

It felt like one of those awful nightmares that you get stuck in and can't wake up from. I looked at the beautiful display of colourful products on the glass shelves, at the bright chiller counter full of delicious fruit, the gleaming granite smoothie bar and the gorgeous old-gold reception desk and comfy purple velvet sofas. My heart lurched in my chest.

No, no, NO!

This couldn't be happening, not after we'd worked so hard…

On jerky legs, I walked out.

"Oh, love, don't go. Let's talk about this," begged Mum.

But I just kept going, slamming the door behind me.

I stomped round the streets for a while, thinking about whether to go to Marco's, or Summer's, or walk to the park where I knew Ben was playing footie with some mates. But I didn't feel like seeing anyone. I walked right up to the top of the high street, which made me really thirsty, but I didn't even have the money for a bottle of water, so in the end I had to go back to the flat.

I stormed up the stairs and marched into the kitchen. They were all sitting round the table with mugs of tea in front of them, and I pointedly ignored them as I reached for a glass and filled it from the tap.

"Abbie, I really think we need to talk—" Mum began.

"Why, have you changed your mind?" I snapped.

"No, but—"

"Well, we don't then," I cut in, swishing past the table. I planned to shut myself in my chill-out room with a book and ignore the lot of them. But instead I found myself turning and shouting, "We can't just go back — why can't you see that? What about your new lives, your new friends? What about mine? What am I supposed to do without Summer and Ben? What about me and Marco?"

"And what about your dad?" Mum asked quietly. "You've got the chance to be nearer to him and see him much more. Isn't that what you wanted?"

"Well, of course, but…" I trailed off. I felt tongue-tied. How *would* Dad feel if he could hear me?

I just felt so confused then, and defeated. I didn't want to talk about it any more, so I grabbed a bread roll from the leftover supper bits on the table and hurried to my chill-out room. I put my headphones in and listened to the songs Marco had downloaded for me, read my book, and pretended I couldn't hear my mum and sisters knocking on the door.

Chapter Ten

On Saturday morning I woke up still in my clothes, sprawled over a floor cushion in my chill-out room (well, cupboard) and for a moment I wondered what I was doing there. Then I remembered everything that had happened and, feeling awful, dragged myself off to the bathroom.

I did go down to Rainbow Beauty to get things ready, but I found myself just standing still, looking around me and thinking about giving it all up, and I suddenly knew that I had to get out of there. I texted Summer and half an hour later Jim pulled up outside in their battered Land Rover, just as Mum and Saff were coming in.

"Hi, love. How are you feeling?" asked Mum.

"I'm going out," I muttered.

"Abbie, please..." she began, but I pushed past her out of the door.

Jed was in the front passenger seat so I squeezed into the little back seat with Summer, saying hi to them all in my best, cheery not-about-to-have-a-massive-cry way. Summer and I had a big hug and I found it really hard to let her go, and even harder not to burst into tears.

"So what's up?" she asked, when we broke apart. I was about to tell her but then I realized that if I did that would be it. She'd know our friendship was going to change for ever. I wanted things to stay as they were for a while longer, so I found myself saying, "Oh, nothing. It's just that I knew you were doing your photos at the beach today and we weren't busy so Mum said I could go out."

"Oh, okay. It's just that in your text you sounded a bit..."

A bit what? *Desperate? Gutted?*

I shrugged. "Oh, I was going stir-crazy stuck inside, that's all. I just fancied some fresh sea air."

Devon air, I thought to myself.

* * *

Soon Summer and I were walking along a sunny autumn beach, with a strong breeze blowing my hair into mad styles, watching her brothers fly these massive multicoloured kites. Summer was taking photos of them for her GCSE photography project, and I was stealing glances at her, feeling a horrible ache inside and already missing her, even though she was right next to me.

Then suddenly tears sprang into my eyes and, as hard as I tried, I couldn't hold them back. I did the oh-gosh-the-wind's-making-my-eyes-water thing for a few seconds, but Summer was onto me.

"I knew something was up," she said, pulling me down onto the sand. She sat beside me and put her arm round my shoulders. "Come on, tell me what's going on."

I shook my head. "I don't know how," I muttered.

"Is anyone hurt?" she asked, looking panicked.

I shook my head.

"Has something happened with Marco?"

"No," I sniffled.

Summer squeezed my shoulder. "Abs, you know you can tell me anything. You're my best friend — whatever it is, we can talk about it."

"And you're mine," I choked out. For a moment, I closed my eyes against the tears that were trying to escape and listened to the waves crashing on the shore. Then I fell onto her and burst into huge, shaking sobs. "Mum's moving us all back to London," I said.

She sat bolt upright, looking startled. "What? Why would she do that?"

I explained about the house-sit and how everyone was completely sure we wouldn't have the cash to pay Mr. Vulmer on the eighth, even Grace.

Summer listened without saying a word. I think she was in shock. "But that's crazy," she said, when I'd finished.

But the worst thing was, as I'd been hearing myself speak, it hadn't sounded crazy at all. It had sounded sensible. Sensible, but *wrong* somehow. I couldn't put my finger on why exactly, but it felt very, very wrong.

"You can't go!" she cried. "I can't believe this!"

"I can't believe it either," I told her, "but it looks like it's happening."

"When?" she asked. "At the end of term?"

I shook my head. *If only.* "A week."

She gasped at that. "Oh my God, no!" she shrieked. "You've got to persuade your mum out of it. Tell her how much you want to stay!"

"I have!" I cried, feeling really frustrated. "Course

I have! But she really thinks it's our only choice."

"Don't go," Summer pleaded. "Stay with *us*. At least in term time. Mum will love it, she's always saying how us two are outnumbered by smelly blokes." She was nearly in tears herself.

I peered at her. "Do you think I could? Really?"

"Yeah, course," she insisted. "Mum and Dad think the world of you. We all do."

It was such a kind offer, and I wanted to stay so much that for a moment I seriously thought about it. But I knew deep down that it wasn't an option. Reluctantly, I shook my head. "Thanks, but I couldn't," I told her. "My family has been fractured enough already. The most important thing is for us all to stay together."

"I understand," said Summer. "If it was me, I couldn't do it either, however much Jim snores!" We both smiled a bit at that. "What a nightmare, though," she said then. "What did Marco say?"

I sighed, picked up a pebble and threw it into the sea. "I haven't told him yet."

"Oh, Abs, it'll be alright, you know," she said, pulling me close again.

"I'm just worried that…if we're apart…" I began. But I couldn't even finish my sentence. I could hardly bear to think about not seeing Marco every day, never mind about whether we could make a long-distance relationship work. I leaped up and headed down the beach. I suddenly felt like I needed to walk.

"You two are *meant* to be together," said Summer, jogging along to catch me up. "No amount of distance will tear you apart. You can come down and stay with me any time you like. Every holiday, and then some weekends in between. And I bet Marco would love the chance to be in London all the time, going to gigs and mooching round record shops. You'd probably never get rid of him!"

"Thanks," I said. "I suppose it's only London, not the moon," I conceded.

"Exactly," she said. "And what with me coming up every five minutes to go round Camden Market with you, and Ben wanting you to show him all the Royal Parks, you'll be sick of the sight of us." She tried to smile, but she couldn't stop the tears from falling down her cheeks. As soon as I saw them, it set me off again too.

"Oh, I feel like I could just...I don't know..." I kicked the ground and a spray of pebbles skittered down the beach. "I feel like throwing myself on the floor and having a massive tantrum, two-year-old stylie!"

I knew Summer understood because she took my hand and said, "Try this." She pulled me along the beach and let out a loud war cry. I ran as fast as I could, and shouted as loud as I could, and we ran and shouted until Jim and Jed and the kites were tiny specks. Then, as our legs gave way underneath us, we fell onto our knees on the stones, gasping for breath.

I'd asked Summer if they could drop me in town, so I could go straight to see Marco at the rehearsal studios, where I knew he was sorting out a new set for Headrush's next gig at the cafe. The sky had clouded over and threatening storm clouds had gathered, and as I walked down the road, shivering in just my little jacket, it felt like they were deliberately hanging right over *me*.

When I got to the studios, I was planning to hang round at the back until they stopped for a break, but Marco saw me and immediately put his guitar down, bounded over and dragged me up to the other guys. I said "Hi" to them all and, even though I had the biggest lump in my throat from knowing what I had to tell him, I managed to ask, "How's it going?"

"Great!" Marco enthused, putting his arm round my waist. "We're working on a new song — it's definitely one of our best."

He did a big sweeping gesture towards Tay, who nodded sagely and said, "I thank you."

"Well, if you're busy, I'll just catch you later," I began, getting that feeling I'd had with Summer too, of not wanting to tell him, of wanting things to stay the same.

"Course not. I've always got time for you, Abs," he said, smiling at me and giving me a kiss on the lips, while the other guys pretended not to notice. "Do you want to hear it? Yeah, let's go for it!" he cried, and did a big American-type whoop. He seemed a bit manic and over the top, not his usual self. And hang on…wasn't Luke supposed to be down here watching? That's what Marco had told me, anyway.

"I thought your dad was coming down," I said.

Marco's cheerful façade slipped then — just for a moment, but long enough for me to see the hurt underneath. "Oh, him? Nah, he left town again. Usual story. Boring old story," he said quickly. "So, let's give this song a go——"

"Oh, Marco, I'm so sorry——" I began, but he cut me off.

"It's no big deal. I totally expected it."

I peered at him. I knew he hadn't. I knew that this time he'd really believed Luke had changed. That he was sticking around. I felt really hurt for him — I knew that under all the bravado he was wondering what on earth had happened, maybe asking himself what he'd done wrong. "But all the plans he talked about…" I began. I felt terrible. I should have stayed on my guard with Luke. Just because my dad had deserved another chance, I'd come to believe that Luke had too.

"Look, of course I wasn't happy about it," he mumbled, "but I've had a chat with Mum, and I know that the people who matter are the ones who are really here for me. Her, you, my mates." He leaped over to Chaz, still in manic mode, and did the big back-slapping bloke thing with him, and then with Tay and Declan.

OMG, now I had to tell him about London. I almost didn't. But then I remembered that Summer knew, and Jed and Jim. I couldn't keep it from him. That felt worse, somehow.

I took his hand. "Let's go outside," I said. "I've got to talk to you about something."

He grinned at me. "You can say anything in front of these guys. They're like brothers to me," he said. Cue more of the back-slapping, man-hug stuff with

Chaz, who was nearest. He was *so* going over the top to try and prove he wasn't that bothered about his dad leaving again.

"No really. Let's go outside," I said.

Fat drops of rain were now spattering the gravel of the car park. I took a deep breath and went for it. "Mum's moving us back to London," I half-whispered. "Next Sunday. For good."

He didn't say anything. He just looked at me, completely bewildered and confused.

And then he walked away.

I dashed after him, calling his name, but he didn't turn around. Instead, he sped up.

I couldn't give up. I kept following him and I was almost at the bridge when the storm broke. There was a big crack of lightning, and then a boom of thunder as a huge black cloud opened above me. The rain pounded down so hard it was like someone had turned on a cold shower over my head, making me shiver and gasp for breath as I tried to run, feet slipping in my (well, Saff's) red ballet pumps. When I wiped the rain from my face, my fingers were covered in inky black mascara. I couldn't see Marco any more, but I had an idea where he might have gone. I ran across the grass on Vire Island – well, squelched across it – looking left and right, trying to shield my face enough to see. There was a man walking his dog, head down, making for home, and a woman shaking a rain cover out to put over her double buggy, but no Marco.

The rain began drumming down even harder then, and I squealed and tried to shield my face with my arms. I felt panic rising up in my chest and I just stood there, getting soaked, until someone rushed up behind me, grabbed my hand and pulled me over to the tea stand.

"Marco!" I gasped, falling into him.

We huddled under the awning at the side of the stand.

"Are you okay?" he asked, shrugging off his jacket and putting it over my shoulders like he had with his blazer, in the storm, the first time we met.

"Are *you*?" I gasped.

"Course not!" he cried. "Dad leaving, and now you—"

"But I don't *want* to go! I'm not *choosing* to go!" I cried. "Mum's made her mind up."

He kicked the ground. "Well, tell her you're *not* going!"

I sighed. "I can't! You know how things are at Rainbow Beauty. She's sure we can't get the money for our rent in time."

"But what about your big pamper day?" he asked. "Surely that will—"

"It won't be enough," I said. "Not even close. Looking at the figures, well, I hate to admit it, but I can see why Mum's doing this."

"But you don't have to go. You could stay with Summer," he argued.

I shook my head. "She did offer, but I can't. My family has been through so much lately – whatever happens, me, Mum, Saff and Grace have to stick together. I can't leave them."

"You're *not* leaving them," he cried. "They're leaving you!"

"You don't understand," I said.

"Yes, I do. I understand that you don't care about staying with me," he said quietly.

"It's not like that," I insisted. "They're my family. We *have* to stay together. We just *have* to."

He sighed. "I'm sorry. I know…I know it's not a competition." He swallowed and looked at his soggy shoes.

"I talked to Summer," I went on, "and I can come down loads to stay with her and you can come up and see me all the time. We can make definite plans. It's not like with your dad—"

"It's got nothing to do with my dad!" he snapped,

looking really upset. "Don't bring *him* into this! This is about you and me. It sounds like you're not even trying to fight this. It's like you don't even care!"

"Course I do!" I half-shouted. "I've argued with Mum, but I can see her point. Not that I've admitted that to *her*. It's true, though – we don't have the money, we're getting chucked out, and there's a rent-free house going... What would *you* do?"

He pulled me into a hug then. "Sorry, sorry..." he said, into my hair. "I know it's not your fault. I know you need to stay with your family. It's... I just... Abs," he murmured, "this is a nightmare. We're meant to be together."

"I know!" I cried. "And I also know that nothing – not time, not distance, not other people – *nothing* is going to tear us apart."

"That's how I feel," he said. He pulled away so he could gaze into my eyes. Suddenly he looked so determined. "I'm not losing you. So what if you go to London? So what if you go to the moon? Nothing is going to break us up. I've never felt this way before. I've never been in love with anyone before..."

I stared at him, my heart pounding.

"I love you, Abbie," he said.

I hugged him tight. "I love you too," I whispered.

201

And then I kissed him. And he kissed me back.

And the rain drummed down all around us.

A little while later, the storm ebbed away and the sun came out, making everything twinkle with raindrops. I took a deep breath as we emerged from under the awning. I love that after-the-rain smell — it makes everything feel fresh and new again.

Then I saw the rainbow.

Marco grabbed my hand. "Come on. Let's find the end! There's meant to be a pot of gold, isn't there?"

"You're mad!" I giggled as I let him pull me along, both of us slipping and sliding on the wet grass. We had to give up when we reached the far edge of the island a few minutes later, because the rainbow's end seemed to disappear somewhere on the other side of the river.

"We'll never reach it now," Marco sighed. "Not without a boat, anyway."

I pulled him close. "It's the trying that counts," I said.

And then I kissed him again. And even though nothing had changed, everything suddenly seemed much, much better.

* * *

When I got in, I still didn't want to talk to Mum, so I went straight to my chill-out room and shut the door. Later on, I came out to get some toast and go to the bathroom. I could have marched right off again, but instead I sat on the arm of the sofa while Mum and Grace were watching telly. Even though I was still really upset, I sort of wanted to be with them too. I didn't say anything, though, apart from at one point, when Grace asked if I wanted a cup of tea.

"Yeah, I suppose so…if you're making it," I told her, and that was it.

Mum sighed and shuffled and looked like she was going to start on about the move again a couple of times. At one point she said, "Abbie, I do need to talk to you about your new school…" But I just glared at her so hard that she must have realized it wasn't a good idea to carry on. Then I went back into my chill-out room and read my book and listened to Marco's music until they'd gone to bed.

When I was sure they were all asleep, I crept out, took the Rainbow Beauty keys from the hook and went downstairs to the parlour. I locked the door behind me and sat in the dark, with only the glow from the street light coming in through the window, bathing the beautiful smoothie counter and shelves of gorgeous products and pretty gold reception desk in a pale orange light. After a while I got chilly and huddled under a pile of towels. And then I started crying and I just cried and cried and cried. Every time the tears stopped, and I thought that was it, more welled up and came pouring down my cheeks. I couldn't believe it was all over.

My dream, our dream, was over.

I woke up on the purple velvet sofa, under the pile of towels, stiff and sticky in my clothes from the day before. For a moment I couldn't remember why I was there, or why my eyes felt bleary and bee-sting puffy, and then it all came flooding back. I was desperate for some fresh air, and for a moment I thought about just going straight out without leaving a note, but deep down I knew I couldn't let Mum worry about me like that, so I crept up to the flat and scribbled on the back of an envelope that I was going to—

I paused – where *was* I going to?

Then I knew. Of course I did. I was going back to my own special place. Vire Island.

* * *

It was almost deserted, apart from a few dog walkers and joggers (and one dog-jogger, weirdly). The tea stand was closed up, unfortunately. There was an early-morning chill in the air and I'd been telling myself that I'd get a nice, steaming-hot cup of tea with my last bit of change as soon as I got there.

I sat on my favourite bench and stared at the river, watching the weeping willows swish in the breeze. After a while, I started to feel a bit better about everything. I knew that Mum really did think she was doing the best thing for all of us, and that Grace and Saff probably believed that too. I didn't — but as I turned things over and over in my mind, I still couldn't see any other solution.

As I sat thinking, I found myself staring at someone on a bench right by the river. It looked like he was birdwatching. What a sensible person, I thought, to bring a flask. And to wear that warm knitted hat, even if it *was* a bit geeky. I blinked at the hat. I *knew* that hat. It was Ben's hat — the blue beanie one he usually wore when he didn't have a scary pink loo-roll cosy on his head. I stood up and was about to hurry off, thinking that I didn't feel up to talking to anyone. But then I realized that he was one of the few people I actually *did* want to talk to.

I sneaked up behind him, lowered his binoculars

and put my hands over his eyes. "Guess who?" I said.

"That perfume…" he said. "It can only be Abbie."

I lifted my hands and he turned and grinned at me. "What are you doing here?"

I sighed and flopped down on the bench beside him. "Avoiding my family," I said. And then I told him why.

He was gutted, of course, and shocked, and for a while he pretended to have spotted something vital in the bird department and wouldn't take the binoculars off his eyes. I pretended I believed him, because it gave me time to sort myself out a bit, too.

"I'm really going to miss you," he said at last, lowering the binoculars and blinking a lot. "I know I'm not Summer, or Marco…"

I nudged his arm. "You mean *so* much to me – I hope you know that," I told him. "I mean, who's going to buy me iced buns now?"

"Cheeky mare," he said, giving me a sad smile.

"I get why they're doing this," I said then. "They think it's the only option."

"And what do *you* think?" he asked me.

"I think…I can see all the reasons to go, logically, in my head. But in my heart…I suppose it feels like giving up…" I paused.

"Go on," Ben prompted.

"Well, I want Mum and my sisters to see that the Rainbow Beauty parlour is more than just a business premises," I told him. "I want them to realize that it's been a magical place for us to come together as a family, to heal our hurt feelings, to find new confidence. That it can be that for our clients and friends too. For the whole community. I keep thinking there *has* to be a way to save it…there just *has* to be. But then my brain kicks in and I think, *How are we going to get two grand by next Saturday?*" I sighed. "I just *can't* face letting Rainbow Beauty go."

Ben stared out at the river for a moment. Then he turned to me and said simply, "Well, then, don't."

"What?"

He shrugged. "Don't let it go. There must be some way of raising the money…"

"We've been round and round that and I really don't think there is," I said. "And, anyway, it's not just the money. There's the new spa to worry about, and we totally messed up the London side of things…" I stopped, realizing I was being just as negative as my mum and my sisters. "You're right," I said slowly. "I *had* given up, just like the rest of my family."

Wasn't Rainbow Beauty worth more than that?

After all we'd been through, shouldn't I fight to the very end to save it? I felt a rush of positive energy race through me. "But I'm back on the case now," I said then. "I'm not giving up until we are *actually* being thrown out on the street by Mr. Vulmer. I'm going to come up with a plan if it kills me."

"That's more like it!" said Ben.

"You're very wise, for a boy," I said, with a smile. "It's almost like, I don't know…like you're not a proper bloke."

He stood up and sat back down with his legs wide apart, and wiped his nose on the back of his hand before pointing at a pair of birds in the nearest tree and saying, "Nice tits."

"Ha ha!" I said, swatting him one. "Seriously, though, if you're so determined and motivational when it comes to my life, how come you don't go for the things you want in your own?"

He raised an eyebrow at me. "I have no idea what you're talking about," he said primly, before putting the binoculars up to his eyes again.

"Oh, I think you do," I countered. "Lovely autumn we're having, by the way. Shame *summer*'s over, though."

Then I winked at him, got up and flitted off.

"Bye!" he said, raising an arm, but not turning

round. Then he called out, "Hang on, are you still doing the pamper day? I'm handing out drinks, aren't I?"

"Yup," I told him. Then an idea shot right through me, rocking me to the core, as if I'd been struck by lightning. "Oh, Ben…that's it!" I cried.

He turned then and said, "*What*'s it?"

I grinned at him. "I'll tell you tomorrow at school!" I called out. "And thanks!"

When I got back in, there was still no one up so I screwed up the note I'd left. About ten minutes later, I was sitting at the table with a mug of steaming tea, scribbling away in my notebook. Mum peered through the doorway and I snapped the book shut. "Is it safe to come in?" she asked. "Or are you going to throw that at me?"

I managed a little smile. "Sorry about yesterday." I wrinkled up my nose. "Erm, and Friday. I *do* understand why you think what you think, even if I don't agree with it."

Mum looked so relieved at that, I thought she might cry or something. But instead she gave me a small smile and said, "Can I push it a bit and ask if we can talk about your new school? I think it might help you feel better about things."

I shrugged. "Sure." She went to get our laptop to show me the school website, and she pointed out all the art and music and stuff they do and we had a good look and I nodded and smiled away. And yes – it looked okay. But inside I was determined – I wasn't *going* to any new school.

I wasn't going anywhere. None of us were.

I was staying right here, and saving Rainbow Beauty. If everyone else in my family had been ground down so badly that they didn't believe they could save our dream, well, then I'd just have to believe in it enough for all of us.

Chapter Eleven

I'd thought about my plan while making Massimo's shower gels and the Rainbow Gift Set orders at the kitchen table on Sunday, and I'd thought about it in the bath, and while I was writing up the refraction stuff in my Physics book. By the next morning, I was ready to get my friends on board. At break time, I dragged them out of the dining hall and onto the field. There was a chilly breeze, but at least it was quiet, and I could see in all directions, so there was no chance of Grace accidentally hearing anything.

"This had better be important!" said Ben, giving me a cheeky smile. "I didn't even get a chance to buy an iced bun!"

"Here, have an apple," said Summer, offering him hers. "You could do with eating more healthily – your skin's been looking a bit dull recently."

"Cheeky cow!" cried Ben, shoving her sideways. Summer shoved him back, then went to eat the apple herself but he grabbed it and took a big bite. "I didn't say I didn't want it," he spluttered, spraying juice everywhere.

"Er, gross…keep your spit to yourself!" Summer shrieked.

"So, what's up?" asked Marco, linking his fingers with mine as we walked along.

I squeezed his hand. "I'm not leaving," I told them all. "Instead, us four are going to raise the rent money and save Rainbow Beauty."

Ben stopped munching the apple and Summer stared at me. "But how? It's loads, isn't it?"

"£1438, to be precise," I told her.

"Abs, I'm desperate for you to stay here – we all are," said Marco. "And we want you to keep your business and everything you've worked for. But, I have to ask… How on earth are we going to get that kind of money? And in less than two weeks?"

"I've had a few ideas," I told him, pulling him down onto the grass. Summer and Ben sat down too (a little closer to each other than strictly necessary, I thought). I pulled out my notebook. "We're going to expand the pamper day," I told them. "Sell twice as many tickets, and have stuff going on out the front, and make up goodie bags to sell. And we'll have a big raffle, so we'll need to get round to local businesses and see if we can get hold of some prizes. Something else we're going to do is sell Rainbow Beauty stuff to girls at school. I can't give them all the *exact* things they wanted, but I'm going to bring in loads of the stock we still have and set up a sales table in the dining hall at break time, hopefully tomorrow. If some people haven't got the money on them, they can bring it in on Wednesday – we can keep a list of who owes what. I've made a list of the girls who've already asked me for things, so we can find them today and tell them about the stall, and get them to spread the word in general."

My friends just stared at me.

"Wow, that's amazing, Abbie," said Summer. "You're serious about this, aren't you?"

"Deadly," I told her. "Now, we need to work out who's doing what. Any more ideas also welcome."

"Me and the band could put on a lunchtime gig in the hall," said Marco. "Charge everyone a couple of quid to get in."

"Great," I said, scribbling it down. "Talk to Mrs. Leavis at form time, yeah?"

Marco winked at me and said, "Consider it sorted."

"You said that you needed stuff going on out the front of Rainbow Beauty," said Summer. "Mum could have a cake stall and I bet her gardening club would provide plants to sell too. I'll ask her when I get home. And I'll set up the product-samples stall here at break with you tomorrow and help you take the orders," she added.

"Fab," I said, glancing up to grin at her as I scribbled it all down.

"I'll go round and ask for raffle prizes," said Ben. "I'm sure I can charm a few lady shopkeepers into parting with their wares." He put on a smooth smile and wiggled his eyebrows.

"In your dreams," said Summer, poking him in the ribs.

"In *yours*, you mean!" said Ben.

"*You* wish!" Summer snorted.

I wanted to shout, *Oh, for goodness' sake, do us all a favour and get together!* But I stopped myself and just said, "Thanks, Ben." I'd had a plan for how to sort *those two* out as well, actually, but it would have to wait for the moment.

"Summer, can you make up some excuse so your dad has to drive us both in to school tomorrow?" I asked then. "I don't want Grace to see the boxes of products, and anyway, I'll need a lift because they're quite heavy. If we go late she won't jump in with us – I know she likes to meet Maisy and Aran in the library the second the doors open. She's always making me come in early."

"Yeah, sure," said Summer. "Don't you want your family catching on to this, then?"

"Of course I'd love to tell them," I explained, "but I'm worried that if I do they might put a stop to it. They won't believe that we can do it until I actually put the money in Mum's hand, so we'll keep it between us until then, yeah?"

"I understand," said Summer.

"Let's say the Headrush gig is to raise money for a new amp," said Marco.

"Good thinking," I said.

"Grace will probably see us doing the product sales, though," Ben pointed out.

"Well, I picked first break tomorrow because she's got Maths Club," I said, "so hopefully she won't, but if she does, I'll just tell her I'm selling a few things to some friends before I go, because I promised them. And I'll persuade her not to tell Mum."

"Abbie, do you really think we can do this?" Summer asked.

"Honestly? I'm not sure," I said. "It's a lot of money. But we're going to give it our very best shot!"

She put her hand out. "We *can* do it," she said solemnly. Ben put his hand on hers, and then Marco did the same, and finally I put mine on top.

"Go, Team Rainbow Beauty!" I cried, and we all whooshed our hands up in the air.

"Go, Team Rainbow Beauty!" Marco echoed. "Oh, but hang on. Couldn't we be called something a bit more manly?"

Mrs. Leavis was completely behind our product sales idea, and cleared it with Mr. Dean the head teacher for us. Then she showed us even more support by buying loads of stuff herself during Tuesday break in the dining hall, and so did Mrs. Lurman, our old form teacher. Summer and I had a queue of girls before we'd even finished setting up the products on the table and Mrs. Leavis claimed teachers' rights to get to the front before she had to go on playground duty.

Just as we were starting to show off the products and make sales, Ben and Marco appeared, looking very pleased with themselves. They were wearing empty tool belts borrowed from Ben's dad, and now filled the slot thingies with goodies to take out and show girls in the playground.

As they headed off, Ben turned back, pulled two shower gels from the belt and twizzled them round a bit before pretending to shoot them at us. "We'll see you ladies later," he said, in what I assume was supposed to be a Western drawl. "Let's go and lasso us some customers!"

Marco gave me a salute and, with that, they both swaggered off, cowboy-style.

I couldn't help giggling, and Summer just rolled her eyes, but it turned out to be a great idea, as girls were obviously loving the attention from Ben and Marco. Soon they were flooding in to buy things, having already tried samples of hand creams and body lotions, and smelled our lovely bubble bath and shower gels. Most of them didn't have their money on them, but they promised to bring it in the next day, and Summer wrote what they owed on a list.

As for our other plans, everything seemed to be coming together pretty well. Summer had said that Annie was more than happy doing the cake and plant stall, and Ben had been round town on Monday after school and was doing a great job of getting prizes for our raffle. Marco said Sienna was also running a prize draw in the pub she worked in with a huge Rainbow Beauty Gift Set that she'd been in and bought with her own money (bless her!). The Headrush pop-up gig in the hall was all set for Thursday and word was rushing round school about it. At least three different people told *me* about it – like, as if I wouldn't already know!

After lunch on Tuesday we had Media. First of all we sat round one big table, working on the Rainbow Beauty pamper day. I'd told Mr. Mac about it and he'd said it was perfect for the whole group to use as a case study before we got into pairs to come up with our own product, service or cause to promote.

I hadn't told him, or any of the other teachers, that I was leaving (well, *possibly* leaving), and I'd persuaded Mum to hold off from calling the school for a couple more days, telling her it was just so I could enjoy things being normal for as long as possible. I'd asked Marco, Summer and Ben not to say anything to anyone else, either.

So anyway, Jess, Bex, Josh, Alex, Raven, Selima and us lot were coming up with ideas for how to get publicity for Rainbow Beauty. Mr. Mac said a report about the pamper day would be something the local press might like, so we contacted the Totnes magazine and paper, and Ben had the idea of getting it in the Dartington Hall newsletter too.

Selima suggested telling the local news programme, *Out and About*. I wasn't sure it would be a big enough deal for them but Mr. Mac said you never know unless you ask, so Alex rang up and left the info with them, emphasizing that I invented all the products myself and I was only fourteen. Mr. Mac had told him to say that, explaining that we had to think of details that might be especially newsworthy to make our event stand out, so hopefully they'd decide to cover it. We'd sold the original fifteen pamper-day tickets, but I wanted to sell at least fifteen more, so Summer and I started designing a flyer to give out round school for people to pass on to their mums, and Jess and Bex took some for the girls from other schools that they'd see at County Netball training that night. We weren't planning to put any round town, in case the Haven Spa found out what we were doing and did something horrible to spoil it. The leaflet gave details about the pamper day on one side, but the other side was just about Rainbow Beauty, using text and pictures we had from other leaflets, so we hoped it would attract people to book in for treatments too.

When that was all done, Summer and I were allowed to keep working on my pamper day, but everyone else had to come up with something of their own to promote.

Ben announced that he and Marco were doing "recycling" as their topic, making Marco slump in his chair, roll his eyes and groan loudly.

"Ignore him. That's a great idea," said Summer, and I saw my chance to start putting my Ben-and-Summer Plan into action.

"Hey, I know, why don't we swap partners?" I said, as casually as I could. "Summer, you go with Ben."

Summer stared at me, obviously wondering what I was up to. I met her gaze and tried to look like I wasn't up to anything. "I know you'll have loads of ideas for the recycling thing, and it's mainly the running-around stuff left to do on the pamper day," I explained. "I don't need *brains* so much at this point, so Marco will be fine to work with."

"Oh, charming!" grumbled Marco, narrowing his eyes at me. But anyway, he helped me make some more pamper-day tickets and write a press release. And afterwards I dragged him off before Summer and Ben had even started packing up their stuff.

"What was all that about?" he asked, as I marched him down the corridor. "If you want to spend more time with me, you only have to say——"

"Not you and me! Summer and Ben!" I hissed.

Marco gave me a look like I was speaking Japanese. "What?"

"I want to get them together," I told him. "They like each other, I'm sure of it."

Marco looked very surprised. "Ben and Summer? Really?" he said. "I haven't noticed anything." Typical bloke.

I rolled my eyes. "Well, I reckon they're into each other. And you can see they'd be great together."

"Huh," he said, like he'd never even thought of it before – which he probably hadn't.

I sighed and ploughed on. "Now they're doing this recycling project together, they'll *have* to spend time alone. So, what we do is, you tell Ben and I tell Summer that the other one's confessed to liking them, but doesn't dare say anything after the...you know, the..." I blushed bright red then.

"I know," muttered Marco.

Neither of us said *after the beach party*.

"It's all a bit cloak-and-dagger, isn't it?" he said, a moment later. "Why do girls have to make things so complicated? Why can't we just go, 'Oi, you like

221

each other. Get together.' End of."

I rolled my eyes. Honestly, boys. I gave Marco a nudge in the ribs.

"Okay, okay, we'll do it your way!" he muttered. "Girls are mad, though."

A few minutes later, us four were in the canteen. *No time like the present*, I thought. So I announced that I had *that thing* I needed to urgently lend Summer that she'd asked for.

She gave me a blank look and I dragged her off before she could say anything.

"What's going on?" she asked, as I pulled her into the girls' loos.

I braced myself. Show time. "Okay, I'm just going to come straight out with it. Ben. Why do you think he was so keen to work with you in Media?"

Summer peered at me in the mirror. "Was he?"

"Yeah! It was SO obvious. He *jumped* at the chance to swap." I rearranged my little sparkly hair clips as an excuse not to look her straight in the eye. I didn't want her to realize that what I was saying was a little, weeny, tiny bit *not entirely true*.

"But that's just because Marco hardly does anything whereas I'm an excellent student..."

I sighed. "No, it's not. Look, you saw me and Marco talking after the lesson, didn't you?"

"No, but, go on…"

"You have to swear not to act like you know this," I hissed, lowering my voice even though we were alone in there. "He let something slip. Something Ben told him." Pause for dramatic effect. "Ben told him he really likes you."

"Of course he does. We're mates," said Summer. You've got to hand it to her – full marks for acting like she wasn't bothered. But she was blushing, and desperately trying to keep a smile off her face.

"No, he really, really *likes* you, as in capital L," I insisted. "Fancies you, capital F, and thinks you're an Amazing Person, capital A and P."

Summer giggled. "Okay, okay, I Get It, capital I, G and I."

Then Mrs. Lurman popped her head round the door and said that the bell had gone two minutes before. She held the door open for us, so we *had* to head straight to her lesson.

We linked arms and walked quickly down the corridor to get out of earshot. "But why hasn't he said anything?" Summer hissed.

"He made such a big idiot of himself at the beach

party that he thinks he's blown it," I said. "But he hasn't, has he? You still like him, right?"

Summer blushed about a zillion degrees. "Well, I can admit it now that I know *he* likes *me*," she whispered. "Yes, I still like him." Cue some really high-pitched girly squealing. Seriously, there were probably bats in caves a hundred miles away with sore ears.

"I knew it. Yes, *yes*!" I yelled, doing that punching-the-air American thing.

Summer leaped on me and got me into a headlock and hissed, "For goodness' sakes, calm down! Mrs. Lurman's right behind us!"

So then we had to be sensible because we'd reached the classroom and not only was Mrs. Lurman behind us but Ben and Marco were coming towards us.

"Just act normal!" I hissed.

Summer looked at me in horror, blushed crimson and clung onto the classroom door frame (i.e. NOT acting very normal).

"What's up with you?" Marco asked her, as he walked past us into the room.

"Oh, time of the month," said Ben knowledgeably, and followed him in.

I looked at Summer. Her face was twice as

horrified after that. "OMG, Abbie! Why on earth did you say—"

I giggled. "I didn't *say*. He must have *thought* when we went to the loos…"

"Come on, girls!" Mrs. Lurman trilled, shooing us into the room and closing the door. "I'm going to assume this excitement is because of your thirst for knowledge," she added archly.

So we had to wait until the bell went to talk about it again, because we had one of those whole-class-debate things where you all bring your chairs into a circle and try to focus on the Poor Laws of 1834, when your gorgeous boyfriend is sitting two seats away.

Afterwards Summer grabbed me beside the lockers, and by grabbed, I mean actually *grabbed*. She looked in a complete panic as she hissed, "What shall I do? Me and him are working on our recycling project together all week!"

I glanced up and down the corridor for signs of Ben or Marco, then said, "Don't try any of your flirting, you'll terrify him. Just be yourself." Then the boys came round the corner and Summer leaped about five feet in the air and bolted in the opposite direction. That's when I started to feel a tiny bit worried that she'd never go near Ben again and my plan was going to totally backfire.

As Ben was rummaging in his locker, I did a most uncool double-thumbs-up thing to Marco to mean that I'd told Summer and she'd revealed she liked Ben. Then I did a big shrug to mean: *Have you talked to him yet?* And he shook his head and did a shooing-away-with-his-hands thing, meaning: *Scoot, I'm just about to.* So I stuck my tongue out at him and hurried off to meet Grace.

Just as me and my sister were heading off down the road, Marco came rushing up. "Wait!" he called. "Hi, Grace."

"Hi," said my sister, looking bemused.

"I just wanted to tell you…job done," he said to me, looking very pleased with himself. "I just talked to him, once you'd *finally* gone."

"And? OMG, I hope he said he does like her, or I've actually *lied* to her, instead of telling the truth but just kind of switching the timing round a bit…" I gabbled.

Marco smirked. "Well, if you'll let me get a word in…"

I swatted him and said, "Fine. Continue." Then I made a zipping-my-lips sign.

"Erm, what are you two on about?" asked Grace.

"Well," said Marco, "I said she liked him and he was really surprised because he said that after the…

you know…the *disaster* in the holidays, he thought it was a no go. But once he knew she liked him, he admitted that he liked her."

I clutched his arm. "OMG!" I squealed. "That's brilliant!"

"Nope, still no clue what's going on," said Grace, rolling her eyes.

"What did you say? What did he say?" I cried, gripping Marco's arm.

Marco gave me a girls-are-mad look. "I *just* told you."

"No, dipstick, I mean the *actual words*!"

Marco repeated the look, but ramped it up to a girls-are-really-really-nuts level. "I said, 'Abbie's definite that Summer fancies you. She's fit. I mean, not to *me* cos she's like my sister, which would be gross, but you should get in there'. And Ben said, 'Cool'."

"Oh!" said Grace. "Right!"

I shook my head in despair. "A bit lacking in romance, wasn't it? Oh, well, it did the job, I suppose."

We had a quick hug (I wanted to give him a kiss too, but I knew that if I did Grace wouldn't shut up about it the entire way home) and then he went off to band practice. I linked arms with my sis and

227

did a little skip so our steps matched, left, right, left, right.

"Abbie, you haven't been matchmaking, have you?" Grace asked.

"Not really. It was more like just helping things along," I said, with a smile. "I've done all I can do now, though. The rest is up to them."

At home on Monday and Tuesday evenings, I kept quiet about what me and my friends were up to, and I joined in when Mum, Saff and Grace talked about packing, and the new school and college. And when Liam came to see how much stuff there was, to make sure it would all fit in his van, I had to go down to Rainbow Beauty and show him what stock we had left.

As we checked through the boxes, I put on a sad smile, while inside I was struggling to stop myself crying out, "We're not going!" But then, as soon as I'd thought that, I couldn't help wondering, *but what if we are?* Then I felt a huge wave of sadness break over me for real, and I had to make an excuse to go into the kitchenette for a minute and pull myself together before I started crying.

Ben and Summer were flirting like crazy all Wednesday (Summer seemed to have finally worked out how to do it without being too scary) but somehow they managed to concentrate on what they were doing long enough to collect up the money from the girls who'd bought Rainbow Beauty products. We gave out loads of our leaflets in the playground too, and told everyone to get their mums to book in for the pamper day (we still had a few tickets left) or just for treatments in general.

Headrush's lunchtime gig in the hall on Thursday was completely packed out (and *A-Mazing*, BTW!), and when Marco came in late to Geography, he was beaming like a little boy. "We made more than £130," he told me. "I went to get it changed into notes for you by the secretary, and she said you can't walk round with it so you'll have to collect it at the end of the day."

"Thanks!" I hissed. I really, really wanted to hug him so much, and because Mrs. Leavis is so nice, and because she was busy setting up stuff on the laptop, I did.

When people started coming in to English after last break, they all seemed to know that I was leaving (Mum must have called the school, despite me begging her not to, just yet). Amany and Iola gave me big hugs and we swapped email addresses. Then Jess, Bex and Rachel came in and we did the whole hugging-and-address-swapping thing as well, and then Ben's footie mates all started hugging me. I thought it was sweet, but Marco, who'd just come in himself, scowled at them and muttered "Any excuse".

On Thursday night back at the flat we all sat round after supper and double-checked we had everything ready for the pamper day. No one was talking about leaving any more. I think they just wanted to put it out of their minds and enjoy the final few days we still had left in Totnes.

"It's typical that business is really picking up now," said Mum. "I had three new clients just walk in off the street today, and another five people rang to book tickets for the pamper day. We're pushing thirty now, Abbie, double what we originally planned. I think we'd better stop there or we won't have room for them all!"

"I have no idea why it's all picked up," I said, trying not to smile as I thought of us four giving out our double-sided flyers to all the kids at school.

Mum sighed. "Oh, well, it's too little, too late, sadly… But it's nice to go out on a brighter note."

"True," said Saff.

"It means I've managed to put another £160 away

for our rent fund," said Grace, looking up from her homework (yes, she was still bothering to do it, even though she thought she was leaving the school the next day!).

"I don't know why we don't just blow that cash on a massive shopping trip and dinner out," said Saff. "It's not like there's any point saving…"

"No, don't!" I cried, in a sudden panic, and then I had to calm myself down and try to look casual. "I just mean…because we'll need it, won't we? We'll need money when we get to London – for ingredients for products and stuff."

"I agree with you, Abbie," said Grace, giving me an approving look. "It's still vital to save as much as we can."

"You two are so *boring*!" Saff grumbled. "I haven't had anything new in, like, for ever! I'm almost in rags here!"

"Cheer up, Cinders," I said. "I'll make you a cuppa."

It took me a while to do the maths in my head while I made the tea, but I eventually managed to work out that with Grace's extra savings we had £722, and then the gig money brought that up to £856, and the profit from the products we'd sold at school made a total of £970. About half the people who'd booked tickets for the pamper day were paying on the day, too, so altogether, our extra ticket sales would give us another £375 (assuming they all actually came, of course). So that was £1345, and then there'd be product sales on the day, and the raffle and stalls, and goodie bags, and Sienna's draw... Raising the final £655 from all that would be a big ask, but perhaps it might be possible.

"Abbie, love, are you okay?" Mum was asking (for the fifth time, as it turned out).

"Yeah, sure...it's just, you know, it's all..." I began, but then I didn't really know how to finish, because there was so much going on in my head, and I didn't want to accidentally let anything slip about my saving-Rainbow-Beauty plans. Mum didn't seem to know what to say either, and she obviously assumed I was just sad about leaving, so she came over and gave me a big hug.

Friday was my last day at Cavendish High, so when I walked into the kitchen that morning wearing purple sparkly tights, little fingerless gloves and enough eye make-up for *ten* Saturday nights, Mum managed to restrain herself from saying anything. Grace had gone wild too – well, wild for her – with loads of mascara

232

and eyeliner, and stripy tights with her Converse. I loved walking across the playground with her into school, seeing everyone turn and look at us. Shappi and Nicky and the other Marco fans from Year 9 all watched as we swished along, arms linked, just like we had on our first day (except we'd both been wearing our revolting pea-green posh-girl uniforms and hideous brown loafers then). The way Marco looked at me when I got into class was very satisfying too. He stared in a *she-is-my-girlfriend-and-I-lurve-her* kind of way, as Saff would put it (well, sing it).

At last break, Ben and Summer were giving a demonstration as part of their recycling campaign for Media, and they'd put posters up all round the school about it, so there was a big crowd of people gathered to watch, including all of us Media lot obviously, plus most of our class, the Year 9 Fan Club, the band, and Grace, Maisy and Aran. Raven was filming it to create a video for YouTube and Selima was taking pictures for Summer and Ben's leaflet campaign.

Summer had told me that the idea was to create a bit of theatre to get the point across in a memorable way, and they'd certainly done that – they were stood in the middle of a massive pile of stinky rubbish, dressed in blue plastic boiler suits with the hoods up. They'd pulled the string bit tight so just their faces were sticking out.

They started talking about how you can recycle more stuff than you think by putting it all into different plastic bins. The girls at the front squealed as Ben waved the black squidgy banana skins right in their faces before putting them into a compost bin.

Marco and I had been in charge of welcoming people, and showing them where to stand, so we were right at the back by the doors. As we watched Ben and Summer laughing and joking around, making everyone else laugh too, the chemistry between them was obvious. Even in the blue plastic suit, Ben was looking at Summer like she was an absolute goddess (I've always said she'd look great in a bin bag and I guess this was as close as I'd get to proving it).

Marco nudged my arm and when I looked up at him he gave me his slow, lazy smile, making my stomach flip over. I smiled back, feeling the strong connection between us.

Ben and Summer's presentation was brilliant, and they got a huge clap and cheer at the end. The bell went and Marco and I had to head off to class, but when ten minutes had gone by, and Ben and

Summer still hadn't turned up to Chemistry, Mr. Fellowes said Marco and I could go and give them a hand clearing up.

As we reached the hall, I looked in through the safety-glass bit of the door, and they had not cleared up anything at all. Not one bit. Instead they were kissing in their blue plastic suits, surrounded by rubbish and recycling bins. I was about to creep away when Marco peered in too, clocked what was going on, and then, with a cheeky smile, opened one of the doors and shoved me into the hall. I shrieked and grabbed his hand — if I was going to spoil their moment, then so was he!

"Get in there, mate!" he whooped, unromantically.

Summer and Ben leaped apart and then much boy back-slapping went on between Ben and Marco, and I have to admit that me and Summer did do a tiny bit of girly squealing and hugging too. When she calmed down, she told me that Ben had asked her out. As in, not out anywhere in particular, but to be his girlfriend in general.

It was my turn to do Saff's wiggly, chanty dance thing then. Until Summer threatened to lamp me one, that is.

"All set for tomorrow, then?" Marco asked, as we headed back to class after clearing up.

"Yep, all set," I reported. "Just the goodie bags to do, but I can sneak down to Rainbow Beauty and get those done later tonight." Then, out of nowhere, I was suddenly struck with a bolt of pure cold fear. "What if it isn't enough?" I mumbled. "What if we have to leave after all?"

Summer hugged me and then Marco and Ben joined in, wrapping themselves around us. "You won't," said Marco firmly.

I pulled them all close and felt a wave of love for them crash through me. "This *will* work. It *has* to," I murmured into Marco's shirt. "There's no way I'm leaving you guys. No way!"

Chapter Twelve

When I woke up on Saturday morning, it only felt like I'd been asleep for about half an hour, because I'd spent most of the night going through all the last-minute jobs we had to do for the pamper day in my head, and thinking about how much money we still needed. My brain kept asking *What if we don't make enough?* And I had to keep pushing that thought away.

I got dressed in my pink Rainbow Beauty uniform and did my hair and make-up really nicely (well, I needed to do *something* to take the attention off my horrible puffy eyes). I messed my hair up a bit, pulled it into a low bunch on one side and added loads of little sparkles and clips.

The pamper day was starting at ten, so we all trooped down to Rainbow Beauty just after nine. I hadn't been able to find a moment to do the goodie bags the night before – there always seemed to be someone around – so I was hoping to somehow do them secretly in one of the treatment rooms. But then Annie pulled up outside in the Land Rover and she and John began unloading crates and crates of plants. Mum asked what on earth was going on and I knew I'd have to come clean.

My heart was pounding and my mouth had gone completely dry. "I, erm, well, we…that's me, Summer, Ben and Marco…well, we've been trying to raise the rent money," I gabbled. "So we've added to the pamper day a bit…"

"Oh my gosh, Abbie. What have you done?" Mum muttered as she put on a big smile and waved to Annie through the window.

I explained about deliberately supersizing the pamper day, and about the product sales at school, and the gig, and the raffle, and the flyers.

"So that's why business has picked up, and why we sold those extra tickets!" gasped Mum. "And because you did it at school, well, I guess that's why the new spa hasn't got wind of it and retaliated. Abbie, I can't believe this!"

"I wish you'd said," said Saff. "I could have done that round college too, selling the products, I mean…"

"And I could have helped at school," said Grace.

They looked so hurt, it made my stomach flip over. "I'm sorry we kept it secret," I told them. I glanced at Mum. "I just thought that maybe, if you found out—"

"I'd have put a stop to it?" she asked. "Well, I might have done, I admit – I wouldn't have wanted you to get your hopes up. I still don't. It's just *such* a lot of money, and the rent isn't the only reason we're going. There's the new spa—"

"This was exactly what I was worried about," I cried. "You're giving up before it's even over. *Really* over."

"I'm not giving up, Abbie. I'm just being realistic," Mum began.

And we were about to have an argument when Grace cut in. "How much have you made?" she asked.

"With the rent money you've saved up, we've got £1345," I reported. "Including all the extra ticket sales for today."

"So, we need to make £655 on product sales," said Grace, without even thinking about it.

"And the stalls and raffle and goodie bags," I said.

"That's a lot, but it might just be possible," she conceded.

"Even if it is, we're still going back to London," said Mum firmly. "I can't just let Janine down at the last minute, and this doesn't solve the problem of the new spa. Look, it was a nice thought, Abbie, and I'm so proud that you've done all this to try and save the parlour, but it's just not an option."

"But I—" I began.

"I'm sorry, love," Mum cut in. "Look, people will be arriving soon. We'll have to talk about this later. Let's just try and have a lovely day, shall we? Now, I must go and say hello to Annie properly."

And before I could say anything else, she hurried off outside.

Saff put her arm round me. "I'm sorry, Abbie," she said. "What you've done is amazing, and I'm right behind you. Of course we'd way rather stay here, wouldn't we, Grace?" Grace nodded. "But Mum's made up her mind and nothing is going to change it," Saff finished.

Then, massive shocker, Grace hugged me. *Grace*. "It's not over yet," she told us. "Let's focus on making that money — then we'll deal with Mum. So, smiles on, girls, and sell your hearts out!"

I pulled Saff into the hug too, and squeezed my sisters tight. "Even though we don't always get on, you are the two best sisters in the whole world," I told them. "Will you help me put the goodie bags together?"

"Course," they said at once, then cried, "Jinx!" and shook pinky fingers.

So I revealed the stash of mini-products I'd made by splitting down our regular-sized stuff, and we got on with the goodie bags. Then Saff prepared the head massage and nail areas in reception, and Grace restocked the chiller counter with gleaming fresh fruit. By the time Summer breezed in just before ten, we pretty much had everything under control. As I went to greet her, I glanced around and realized that Rainbow Beauty had never looked more beautiful.

A couple of minutes later, Ben came in, and he and Summer hugged and then kissed on the lips and of course Grace did the *oooooh* thing and Saff demanded to know what was going on.

Then Marco slouched in, and he didn't get a kiss on the lips from me, because Mum came out of the kitchenette. "Oh, hi, love," she said to him, then, "Abbie, could you find the product info you took to London and file it with the other cosmetic-testing certificates and things, please, in case anyone wants to know more about anything?" Then she hurried off to get the towels out of the dryer.

"Sure," I called after her, leaving Ben and Summer to finish off the display. The display on the coffee table, that was, not the display of kissing – although they did finish *that* off too.

I rooted around behind the reception desk for the smart pitch bag we'd taken to London. As I pulled the folder out of it, something sticky attached itself to my hand. I freaked out for a moment in case it was a *dead* something and flicked my wrist so that whatever it was fell to the floor. When I was sure that it wasn't living, and hadn't ever been, I picked it up again. It was a sticky, yellow oval thing, now covered in fluff.

A lemon drop.

I stared at it, remembering how Marco had hidden the sweets in my bag so I'd find them when I got to London. One must have fallen in here somehow, when I was sharing them round.

I thought about all the great times Marco and I had had together – hanging out on Vire Island, and at the cafe, and having burgers at Rocket. Working together in lessons (well, okay, *flirting* together in lessons), and chilling out on the field at the end of the summer term. Getting Rainbow Beauty all kitted out and painted ready to open. Saff setting us up, making me give him a man manicure in one of the treatment rooms. Having dinner round his house with his lovely mum. I found myself rushing across the parlour and hugging him tight.

He hugged me back fiercely. "This *will* work," he said into my hair.

Mum hurried over to the door. "Everyone ready?" she asked.

"Yes!" we all cheered, trying to hide our nerves.

"Then let's get this show on the road," she said.

Ten minutes later, Rainbow Beauty was absolutely buzzing with people, inside and out. Annie was doing a roaring trade on her cake-and-plant stall, and Maisy and Aran were very busy selling goodie bags and products out there too.

Saff gave me her tray of fresh juices, as she was due to go and start doing the mini-manicures. I noticed that Jess, Bex and Rachel from netball had come and were already gathered round her little nail station, and I gave them a wave. Mavis from the chip shop in the parade was there too, and Florrie, Tom the greengrocer's wife, was looking at our product samples on the coffee table with Sue from the cafe.

Tom himself came in with a huge box of fruit and

veg he'd donated for the smoothies (Summer had tipped him off), and I watched Liam take the box from him and thank him warmly. I recognized a group of sixth formers from our school, and saw Saff's college tutor chatting to Emily. Emily didn't stay a guest for long, though – she hadn't even finished her smoothie when Saff dragged her over to the nail table to help out, as she already had quite a queue forming.

Marco was put to work too, bringing out the massage table and setting things up for the demonstration. Mum had intended to do it in one of the treatment rooms, but it was clear that there were far too many people to squeeze in there. As he heaved the heavy table past me, Marco looked really pleased with himself, and Summer grinned and said, "Aw, bless him, he's been given a *manly* job at last!"

Grace was already ringing up sales at the till, and she called to me, "Abbie, could you go and find Mum? It's time for the demonstration, and I'm not sure where she's got to."

I found her in the kitchenette, fussing about with the spare cups Annie had brought. "Mum, it's time," I told her.

"Let me just finish this…" she muttered. Then she looked up at me and gabbled, "Oh, Abbie, there are so many people! I wish I hadn't put myself down for this. What if it goes wrong?"

"It'll be fine," I told her. "Just step away from the china. I know you can do this." I steered her back out into reception and over to the massage table.

Liam took one look at Mum's terrified expression and said, "It'll be fine, Kim," and before she could do a runner he pulled her into a big hug. As they broke apart, I spotted three more people arriving. They didn't look like pamper-day guests. For one thing, two were guys. One of them was holding a massive film camera on his shoulder while the other wrestled a boom mic through the door.

"OMG, they came!" I gasped. "The *Out and About* people!"

"Hi, I'm Genna Harris," said the woman, striding over. She was wearing a beautiful green silk dress, and she held out her hand to shake Mum's as she reached us.

"Perfect timing," said Liam. "Kim's just about to do a massage demonstration."

"Not on TV, I'm not!" Mum shrieked, but Liam just clapped his hands together to get everyone's attention, and called out, "Ladies, if you'd like to gather round, Kim will show you the basics of massage technique, so you'll soon be able to give your loved ones a blissfully relaxing experience any day of the week!" Then he pulled his shirt over his head, to huge cheers, put a towel round his waist, wriggled his jeans off underneath it, and lay down on the table.

Mum smoothed down her uniform and hair, and took a deep breath. Then she smiled and said, "So the first thing is to ensure that your client is warm and comfortable..." And then she was off, talking as she was massaging, about key areas that hold tension, and pressure points, and which essential oils are really good for relaxation. After a while she seemed to forget about being nervous, and about the TV crew, and she was just chatting like she would to a room full of friends, and they were hanging on her every word. When she'd finished, she got a huge clap and cheer, and so did Liam (as well as a few wolf whistles!).

Then there was a short break, and I realized with a start that I was up next, to talk about our products. I felt completely overwhelmed, though, looking at the crowd of people, so I persuaded Saff to do it instead. Well, I say *persuade*, I only really had to give her a *help!* look from across the room and she came bounding over, slicking on lip gloss and fluffing up her hair.

She was absolutely brilliant at it, of course, and afterwards, during the buffet lunch, the products she'd showcased started flying off the shelves. She looked so pleased with herself that I thought she might be about to start signing autographs or something, but in fact she got straight back to the nail station. She sat down beside Emily and called the name of the next person on the list (their tutor had helpfully suggested they start one, so people didn't have to stand there waiting for a turn).

"Perhaps the TV show will take you on as a presenter," I said to her a moment later, as I handed over the new can of quick-dry spray and bottle of Black Cherry nail polish they needed.

"Nah, I definitely want to be a beautician now — well, own a chain of beauty shops, anyway, and be flown to Hollywood specially to give treatments to the stars," she added, grinning at me.

I grinned back at her. "You know what? I totally believe that will happen," I said.

I started restocking the glass shelves then, because we were all out of the Spicy Delight Bubble Bath and the Carrot and Calendula Hand Balm (Annie had been singing its praises to everyone). The bowl of orange and lemon star soaps was almost empty, too.

I noticed that the chiller counter was looking a bit bare as well, so Grace popped upstairs to grab the last box of fresh face masks from our fridge.

Mum hurried over with an armful of products someone had chosen and put them on the reception desk. "These are for Mrs. Claridge, the older lady sitting there on the sofa, if you could put them through the till for her, and people have nearly finished their lunch, so we need to get the next round of coffees going, and Jane's asking whether you've got any more of the Rose and Geranium Bath Bombs... Oh, I'm run off my feet!" she giggled, looking happier than she had for ages.

While Saff and Mum were serving the tea and coffee, Grace and I totted up how much we'd made. (Okay, Grace did, and I watched.)

"That's another £302, which makes £353 more to go," said Grace excitedly. "If we can keep selling products and raffle tickets right until the end – and there's the money from Annie's plants and cakes, remember – it might just be enough. And even if we don't have *quite* enough, if Mum agrees to us staying, maybe we can try and save the last bit over the next week..."

"That's fantastic," I began, but then my heart sank into my shoes as the door opened and a familiar

– and very unwelcome – figure in a hideously patterned shirt lumbered in.

Mr. Vulmer.

Mum was walking out of the kitchenette with a tray of coffee cups in her hands and when she spotted our landlord she almost dropped them. "What's he doing here?" she hissed. Shakily, she handed the tray to Maisy and hurried over to us, with Saff hot on her heels.

"If you want a free treatment, you're out of luck!" Saff snapped at Mr. Vulmer as he reached us.

He gave her a nasty look. "I haven't come for a *treatment*," he sneered. "I've come for my rent money."

We were all stunned. "But it's not due until next week!" I stuttered.

"That's not fair!" cried Grace.

Liam appeared by Mum's side then. "What's going on?" he asked her. "Do you want him to leave?"

Mum clutched Liam's arm. "He wants the rent *now*," she murmured.

"We don't have it. Not quite. Not yet," Grace said, as sweetly as she could manage. "If you could come back next week, as we agreed…"

"No can do. I'm off to Malaga tomorrow," he

said. "If you can't pay, well, I'll just give you your notice right now. It's my right."

A hush had fallen over Rainbow Beauty and I realized that everyone was watching us by then, and listening. I really thought it was all over. And glancing at Marco, seeing the pained look on his face, I knew he did too.

Mum took a step towards Mr. Vulmer and smoothed down her uniform. When she began to speak, I was completely sure she'd say, *It doesn't matter. We're leaving tomorrow anyway.*

But instead she drew herself up and looked him straight in the eye. "We're not going anywhere," she announced.

I gaped at her. "But Mum, we don't have—" I began.

"You were right, Abbie," she said, cutting in. "All the magic, all the inspiration for our Rainbow Beauty products...well, it's right here. Things have been so difficult I'd lost sight of that. But I realize now how much support and goodwill we have from the community." She turned to our guests and friends. "From all of *you*. We've *already* settled here, and it feels like home. So, no, we're not giving up, not until the very last minute."

Mr. Vulmer rolled his eyes. "Nice speech and

everything, but this *is* the very last minute. And if you don't have the full amount, I'm giving you notice."

In a daze I leaned down and grabbed the red cash box from under the reception desk. Grace and I had put all the rent money in there and now she unlocked it and showed him the wad of notes. "We're only missing the last £350," she told him. "Well, £353, to be precise. If you could call back in a few hours, perhaps…"

"I told you. It's now or never," he snarled. "And it looks like you don't have the money, so——"

Ben suddenly leaped forward, digging in his pocket. "I want two strips of raffle tickets, so that's the three quid sorted anyway," he said, dropping the coins into the cash box.

I gave him a grateful smile. It wasn't nearly enough, of course, but it was sweet of him.

"I haven't paid for my goodie bag yet," said Annie, stepping forward, "and I'm treating Summer to one too."

"Oh, Annie, that's really kind, but you don't have to——" Mum began.

"Kim, I was planning to buy them today. I just hadn't got round to it yet," Annie said firmly, and pushed three £10 notes into Grace's hand. Grace

251

stared at them, then put the money in the cash box too and smiled.

Mr. Vulmer looked bewildered for a moment, and then he looked very, very angry. "No, hang on. You can't just—" he began.

But he was drowned out because suddenly everyone was crowding round the desk, trying to talk to Mum.

"I'm booking next week's massage," said Trish, "and I'd like to pay now, in advance."

Mum gave her a stern look, but Trish just said, "What? It helps me keep track of my money."

Mum smiled at her. "Thank you," she murmured.

Saff and I started talking to people too, and Grace handled the cash box, and soon lots of others had booked up for treatments and paid in advance, or were insisting on paying for treatments they'd already booked, or were lining up products on the reception desk to buy. Annie had to rush back outside to help John with the cakes and plants, because there was suddenly a rush on those too. For the next few minutes, Mum, Saff and I were just in a frenzy of booking things in and Grace's hands were flicking in and out of the cash box, taking money for sales and giving change. Mr. Vulmer just watched, with his mouth open and his eyes goggling out.

Then Summer hurried over with all the takings from the cakes and plants, which was just over £50, and Grace waved her hand in the air for quiet and handed Mr. Vulmer the red box. "*Now* it's all there," she told him, with a satisfied smile.

Of course, being him, Mr. Vulmer stood there and slowly and deliberately counted it, while everyone watched him. Then he smiled slyly. "It's a tenner short," he announced. "Here, count it yourself."

"What? I'm *never* wrong—" Grace stuttered. But obviously, in all the mayhem, she had been, just a little bit.

The next thing I knew, Marco was by my side, putting a crumpled fiver and a heap of change down on the reception desk. "I want one of those man manicure thingies you demonstrated on me," he told me, then glanced at Mum. "Honestly, I really do," he insisted. "Look, my cuticles are in a terrible state."

Everyone burst out laughing as he wiggled his fingers in the air. As Grace handed Mr. Vulmer Marco's money, another huge cheer went up. I pulled my BOYFRIEND close and whispered into his ear, "I love you, terrible cuticles and all – which I am now going to have to see *every single day*."

"I love you too," he said to me – well, more like

announced to the room. But no one heard — there was way too much hugging and cheering and general celebrating going on. And then there was more laughter as Mr. Vulmer dropped £1 and instead of just leaving it, he got down on the floor and scrabbled around under the sofa for it. The biggest cheer came as he left, slamming the door so hard that the bell almost jangled off its hook.

Suddenly Marco and I were jumped on by Ben and Summer. Emily was still hugging Saff, Maisy and Aran were mobbing Grace, and Liam actually picked Mum up and swung her round and round.

"Yes!" cried Saff, punching the air. "Devon rules, cowpats and all!"

Grace grinned. "Hear that? Saff's signing up for more country walks!"

"Woah, steady on…" Saff began.

"Thank you, Abbie!" Mum cried. "Thank goodness for you! Thank you for seeing the truth and helping me to see it too, before it was too late. Thank you for not giving up, even when it all seemed hopeless."

I grinned. "You're welcome," I said. Then in my head I found myself repeating, *We're staying. We're staying. We're staying.* Each word was delicious — a spell cast, a wish granted, a dream come true.

"Okay!" Mum said, detaching herself from us and turning to address our guests. The room fell silent. "Thank you," she said. "From all of us, our heartfelt, sincere thanks for all your support and friendship. We look forward to being part of this community for many years to come."

She got a huge round of applause then, which made her go all flushed and flustered and grin about a mile wide. "Let's all move over to the smoothie bar and Grace and I will show you the secrets of beauty from the inside out!" she said. "We've got a great new smoothie recipe lined up that's bursting with vitamins for health and vitality. And we'll also demonstrate how to make a quick and easy fresh face mask, because of course, what's good for you on the inside can be great for your skin too."

She grabbed Grace's hand and strode over to the counter, all traces of nerves gone. They stood behind the blenders and Grace said, "So, for this beautiful blueberry smoothie, which is just bursting with antioxidants, you'll need…"

"One punnet of gorgeous blueberries," Mum continued, holding them up.

They gave a great presentation, and everyone got a little cup of the smoothie to try, and a sample of the avocado fresh face mask they'd made to take home.

Soon after that it was almost time to finish, so we did the raffle, and Ben went crazy when he won the luxury handmade chocolates donated by the little sweet shop in town. "Yes! That's three things I've won now!" he whooped. Then he grinned at Summer. "My luck is definitely changing!"

Saff and Emily had just about finished all the mini-manicures by four, when Mum did her last head massage, so we all thanked everyone again for coming and buying and booking so generously.

Maisy finished helping Grace cash up, and then she went over to Ben and Marco, who were handing people their jackets. "When Aran's finished drying up, we'll head off—" she began.

"No way!" cried Liam. "You're not going anywhere! We are going to celebrate! I'll just pop and get some tunes!" And with that, he did a comedy dance out of the door.

Just as the last guest was leaving, with warm hugs for Mum and a promise to come back soon, the phone rang.

I grabbed it and almost-sang, "Good afternoon, Rainbow Beauty!"

It was Dad. "You sound very cheerful!" he said. "How's the pamper day going?"

"Great. Brilliant!" I cried.

"Excellent. Good to hear it," he said. "Listen, do you know when you're getting to the house tomorrow? I was hoping there'd be time for me to come over and see you, before school starts and everything…"

My heart started pounding. Of course, our news wouldn't be good news to Dad. But still, I had to tell him.

I took the phone from the stand and hurried to the kitchenette, where it was quieter. "Dad, we've managed to raise the money to stay here, and Mum's agreed to it," I told him. "I'm so sorry — I know this isn't what you wanted…"

I thought he'd be really upset, or get angry, or maybe just hang up. But instead there was a silence, and then he sighed deeply. "Of course I would have liked you to move back up here, but I want what's best for you all, and I know your mum does too. So if staying is best…then I'm very happy for you."

"That's really big of you," I told him, feeling a surge of love and admiration for him.

"That's being a parent for you," he said. "Although part of me wants to stamp my feet and *insist* you come up here, of course!"

"We'll still see you loads," I assured him. "Someone's got to make sure you're keeping your place up to me and Saff's standards. Oh, actually, I've just had a thought – Janine won't be able to get professional house-sitters at such short notice. I'll ask Mum to suggest you as a replacement when she calls her."

"Oh, yes, please!" said Dad eagerly.

"Then we'll have somewhere nice to stay when we come and see you," I added. "I've recently learned that distance doesn't matter, not when you love each other."

"Oh," he said. "So, hang on, what's this about love—"

"Gotta go, Dad, speak soon!" I gabbled, and hung up the phone before he could ask any horribly embarrassing parental-type questions about me and Marco.

Back at reception, I put the phone down in its stand and went to mention the Dad idea to Mum, who hurried straight off to ring Janine. Then I helped Grace to clear up and sort out the smoothie bar.

As we stacked up the paper cups for recycling, she said, "Seeing this place buzzing today…I mean, we *did* this, Abs, all of it. It makes me feel like I can do *anything*."

"So it's not just Saff who's going for world domination now, then?" I joked.

I felt the same, though, and I was buzzing with new ideas for the business too.

Mum came up a moment later. "I've spoken to Janine," she said. "She was a bit surprised about our change of plans, but she's really happy for us. And she's happy for Dad to stay in the house, too — we've both known her and Peter for years."

"Oh, fantastic!" I cried. "I'll text him in a minute."

"Yes! No more sleeping in that vile saggy old bed!" cried Saff, who'd come over too.

Mum smiled and had begun to walk away when I said, "By the way, I've had some new ideas for the business — we can offer pamper parties in people's houses, and do mini-treatments in retirement homes, and put on a special men's night, and find more events to have a Rainbow Beauty stall at, and then there's the Devon County Show…"

Mum giggled. "Good thinking, Abbie!" she cried. "I just know we'll be okay here now, with you coming up with such great plans. I won't forget what's happened today. Whatever we have to face in the future, however tough it gets, we will *not* give up. Not again. Not ever."

I dashed round the smoothie bar and gave her a big hug then, and Saff and Grace joined in too.

"Go, Green girls!" cried Saff, making us all giggle.

A few minutes later, when the clearing up was finished, I slipped off upstairs to change out of my uniform. When I came down again, I found everyone with blueberry smoothies in their hands, and Summer setting up her camera on the timer to take a picture of us all.

"Abbie, quick!" Marco cried, pulling me in and wrapping his arms around me.

I grinned as the flash went off, then glanced around as Mum, Annie, John, Trish, Liam, Summer, Marco, Ben, Saff, Emily, Grace, Maisy and Aran stopped posing and started chatting. Then we all burst out laughing as the flash went again.

"Got you!" cried Summer gleefully. "The surprise shot's always the best!"

Half an hour later, the party was in full swing. Liam's "tunes" turned out to be "Celebration" by Kool and the Gang on a loop. He'd got fish and chips from Mavis's place for us all, and he and Mum were working their way through a bottle of champagne and threatening to chronically embarrass me by playing Twister. Jim, Summer's older brother, had come to get a lift home and ended up joining the party. Now he was dancing with Saff, who'd sneakily put on a fast song to get him up, and then changed it to a smoochy one once she'd got hold of him. It was "Make You Feel my Love" by Adele. Not big on subtlety, my sis.

When the music slowed, Summer dragged Ben onto the dance floor (well, the area where the sofas had been pushed back), and I looked at Marco and raised my eyebrows. He held out his hand, and pulled me into his arms. "I can't believe you're staying," he said, as we swayed together. "It's perfect."

"Your perfect life!" cried Summer. "Personally, I think your taste in boys is a bit dodgy, but—"

"Oi. This is a private conversation!" said Marco.

I giggled. "Everyone knows slow-dancing with boys is just an excuse for girls to chat to each other, right?" I leaned to the left so I could see Summer. "It's true. I've got everything I could wish for," I said to her. "So, if I had *another* Blueberry Wish, I'd just wish for things to stay as they are…oh, except to grow the business more, of course, and to get my own bedroom, and to stop being headless…"

Ben rolled his eyes. "Girls…they're never happy!" he groaned.

"Hey!" cried Summer, and swatted him one, so he danced her into a wall.

Then Mum called out, "Right, that's enough of you teenagers mooning over each other!"

We all burst out laughing and Saff said, "Mum, I think *mooning* probably meant something a bit different in your day!"

Mum raised her eyebrows. "I'm still down with the kids," she said. "How about this?" And with that she put on a Korean horse-riding-based party song (ha ha!) and dragged Saff, Grace and I over to dance with her. As we bounced around, giggling, my head swam with all the colours surrounding us, and all the friendship, fun and laughter. And I knew for sure that our dream really *had* come true. We were in that magical place, that place *somewhere over the rainbow*.

Our new beginning had become our happy ending.

The End

Turn the page for a yummy

Rainbow Beauty

recipe, an exclusive author

interview and MORE!

Blueberry Wishes Smoothie

Mixing up a *Rainbow Beauty* fruit smoothie
is a fun, fast and yummy way to help ensure you're
eating lots of fresh fruit – perfect for feeding your
skin and hair with all you need to give you that
gorgeous glow.

Always remember the
Rainbow Beauty motto:
*Beauty from the
inside out!*

You will need:
1 banana
150g (5oz) blueberries
150g (5oz) natural
yoghurt

If you don't have
a jug-style blender,
use a handheld
blender instead.

1. Peel the banana and cut it into thick slices. Rinse the blueberries and dry them on a paper towel.

2. Put the fruit in a jug-style blender with the yoghurt and whizz together until smooth. Then kick back, relax, and enjoy!

To make this an extra-special *Rainbow Beauty* smoothie, you can pop in some raspberries for a bigger burst of fruity goodness. Or for something a little bit sweeter, why not try adding apple juice or a dash of runny honey? Delish!

For more mouthwatering recipes that are perfect for parties, sleepovers and girly nights in, check out

ISBN: 9781409532767

Collect every gorgeous
Rainbow Beauty book!

ISBN: 9781409539605

Abbie's life feels like one big rain cloud since
her parents split up. Now she lives with her mum and
sisters in a grotty flat. Only new friends, Ben, Summer,
and gorgeous, guitar-playing Marco, offer
Abbie a silver lining.

But then Abbie has a bright idea to turn her family's fortunes
around. She's always loved making her own luscious beauty
products. Could opening a new business – the Rainbow
Beauty parlour – bring her family a pot of gold and heal
their hearts too?

ISBN: 9781409540557

School's out for the summer holidays, but there's no stopping
Abbie. With business booming at her family's exciting new
venture – the Rainbow Beauty parlour – and
heart-throb Marco whisking her off on dates,
life is one big whirlwind.

But while Abbie longs to see Dad again, everyone else
thinks he should be left out in the cold. Will Abbie's summer
be filled with sunshine and strawberries, or are there
storm clouds up ahead?

Also available as ebooks

A girly chat with
Rainbow Beauty
author
Kelly McKain

Blueberry Wishes starts with Abbie going back to school. What was your favourite subject?

English! I loved reading and writing, and talking about books and poems. And History and Spanish. I'm afraid I was a total Hermione at school but, like Abbie, quite bad at Maths!

The students have to devise a product for Media class. What would your new invention be?

Erm, Dog-Nav, so you know where they have gone when they bolt off chasing rabbits. And maybe dog treats with a long-range smell-activation so you could get them to come back again straight away. And some way of keeping pairs of socks together. And self-making beds... And self-cleaning children... I could go on...

This book has such a cosy autumnal feel. Which season do you enjoy the most?

The turn from summer to autumn is my favourite part of the year. I love the back-to-school feeling (see my Hermione-ness!) and the way the air changes and everything smells different, with more golden sunlight and all the gorgeous falling leaves.

What is your favourite Rainbow Beauty product from this book?

It's gotta be the Blueberry Wishes Face Mask – I might have a go at making some of that, actually! And I've always loved the sound of the Carrot and Calendula Hand Balm, too.

Abbie, Summer, Saff and Grace all have a very individual sense of style. How would you describe yours?

I'm totally into skater dresses at the moment, and wear them all year round, either with ballet pumps, or with black leggings and boots. And I couldn't be without my battered old leather jacket, which seems to work with pretty much everything else in my wardrobe.

In the series, Abbie changes from a glam city girl to a laidback country chick. But which one are you?

Ha ha! Good question! Like Abbie, I'm a bit of both. I'm just about to hop on the train to London, but this morning I was deep in the woods walking the dogs. So I'm lucky – I've got the best of both worlds.

Vire Island is such a special place for Abbie. Where's your favourite place to be?

Anywhere where there are trees, I'm happy. I love the woodland and heathland where I live, and Chiswick House Park in London. I also love Lazienki Park in Warsaw – I've only been there twice but it's very, very special.

Abbie's friends are so ingenious in helping to raise the cash to save Rainbow Beauty. If you had to hold a fundraiser, what would you do?

Maybe a sponsored silence cos my family and friends would know how massively hard I'd find that and sponsor me loads. Or a vintage fashion show – that would be fun!

So, we know Liam's a big fan of "Celebration" by Kool and the Gang, but what's your ultimate celebration song?

Anything that makes me go *Woo-hoo, yeeeaaahh!* when it comes on! I put on Katy Perry or Adele to celebrate finishing writing a book (or just a chapter or scene — any excuse to get up and dance around).

Imagine Abbie in ten years' time. What do you think she'll be up to?

Back from her travels around the world learning the beauty secrets of different cultures? Engaged to Marco? Running the London branch of Rainbow Beauty with Saff? You decide!

For all the latest news from Kelly, check out

www.kellymckain.co.uk

Calling all Abbie fans!

For exclusive Rainbow Beauty material
log on to

www.kellymckain.co.uk/rainbowbeauty

Join in with all the latest
Rainbow Beauty chat online

Be the first to know about
Rainbow Beauty competitions and giveaways

Download gorgeous Rainbow Beauty
screensavers and friendship vouchers

Learn how to do your own DIY manicure
– perfect for that Saturday sleepover

Discover Kelly's fave pampering treats

And lots, lots more!